THE UNLOUNGING

FROM
A BELLY FULL OF BEER TO
A CRAW FULL OF
TIME

BY
SELRAYBOB

Published by Cur Dog Press
Austin, Texas
CurDogPress.com

ISBN-10: 0-9846156-6-0
ISBN-13: 978-0-9846156-6-7

Contents

Acknowledgements

A lot of people helped me put this together. Of course there's Susy Liu Anne and Herm, without whom I might still be on the lounger, but other people helped too, with lots of things, for a long time. But if I went through all my life, thanking all the people who'd helped me, I'd have to include the guy who put my first bicycle together and the coach who'd taught me how to block. So I'm going to keep it to the people who helped me put this book together. And I'm going to put the names in alphabetical order by first names, because you all matter to me. So besides Susy Liu Anne and Herm, who are worth mentioning twice, thanks also to Andrew Novick, Cheryl, Cindy, James Burris, Jason, Joalene (yes, really), John Lowe, Rachel F, Roger, and Stewart.

For those who feel like roadkill,
but aren't dead yet.

THE UNLOUNGING

FROM
A BELLY FULL OF BEER TO
A CRAW FULL OF
TIME

1

No Good Time to Lose a Wife

I was sitting by the window, quart of Busch on my belly, when my wife Joalene walked in and commenced to tell me that I'm a witless, no-good, washed-up nothing and how I'm never going to amount to even a worm on a pile of mole scat if I spend all my time sitting on the lounger and drinking beer—which, just to be clear, I was not drinking, since it was on my belly. But while Joalene was talking, just as she said the word *time*, instead of looking out the window at the leafless oak like normal, I looked at the clock. And I started thinking about the black marks on the white face and the hands and how they go round and round and round and round and what that means now that we have digital clocks, one of which was on the top of the movie recorder. So I looked over there. The red numbers were 9:45, and the circular clock, as close as I could tell, was pointing at 9:38. So while Joalene was breathing in, which she almost never seemed to do, I asked her if she had seven minutes I could have. "Because I'm thinking," I said, "that if you would just move over a bit, so as I can't see the clock there that says 9:45, then it will only be 9:38, and I'll have seven more minutes to sit here with my beer, and maybe drink some, and then, if you don't mind so much, sweetheart, you can get me some lasagna from out of the fridge."

She scowled and spun around. Her hair went swooshing past her neck, and she went swinging those delicious heart-shaped hips of hers into the bedroom and then back out a couple minutes later with her hair curled, eyes done up all blue and hot, and her lips puffed out showing teeth smudged red with lipstick in the way that used to make me want to jump up and start mashing my tongue into her mouth to clean them off. But it didn't work that way anymore. She'd become the errand woman and me the pizza eater.

Now that's no way to think about your high school cherry turned wife. I knew it, too. It's crap. But when I looked at her parading herself back and forth for me, trying to get me going in that malicious way of hers, I didn't think about us driving up to St. Louis to get her now dearly-departed toy poodle Lexie, or barbecuin' quail by the river and sitting naked later and giggling.

No. I thought that she was wasting my time, and where was she going, and why wasn't she getting me that lasagna? And if she was just going to flaunt herself at me and not come over close so as I could smell her, then she may as well call the pizza man and order us a large pepperoni.

I didn't say anything, though. She may have been parading, but she was scowling while she was doing it. And even with this acorn I got in my head, after eight years you learn when to shut up. And sometimes you actually do.

So I looked at the clock again, at the circular one with a second hand that goes round and round, tick by tick, then back to the skirt hugging Joalene's curves and back to the red numbers and back to Joalene as she walked back into the bedroom and slammed the door. I caught myself sitting up and listening and wondering whether she was packing or undressing or adding another coat of gloss to her lips. But I sure wasn't going to have her burst out and catch me gawking at the light under the door. So I went back to staring at the clock. I almost got myself hypnotized watching the second hand go round and round, which would've been good, I tell you, to keep my thoughts from turning on. Because unfortunately, they did. I caught the red number clock flip four to five, and it got me to wondering why one time is right and another is wrong and why one is fast and another slow. Why do we even watch the clocks, and who decided what a minute is anyway?

Of course, then Joalene came out with her yellow suitcase, hand-painted with red flowers—by her, with the paints I'd bought—and planted her heels in the vinyl brick of the entranceway and glared down at me and said, "I've waited long enough for you to make something of yourself. I have. A long time, Selraybob."

After she said that, I said, "Eight years."

"*EIGHT YEARS!*" she yelled. "And you've become fatter and fatter and less and less." And I had, I admit. I'd tried plumbing school a few years back, thinking all that bending over and getting up would slim me down, but two weeks in, I flooded a funeral home with a backed-up toilet. After that came furniture moving with my friend Herm. But not three days after the fatal encounter between little Lexie and the blind man with the spiked cane, Herm and I dropped a dresser on a two-pound Chihuahua. Two dead dogs in three days. It was rough. Tearful even. I took it as a sign to ease back on the physical strain. So Joalene was right. "It's a long time to wait, Sel. It really is."

I hate to say it, because she sounded a little sad, but instead of looking at her while she was talking at me, I was checking the clock and counting. And the next thing I did was ask her, "Joalene," I said. "What is this thing 'time' you keep talking about, and does it really make sense to wait, or have you just been working a whole lot on improving me while I've been doing a good deal of sitting on the lounger and enjoying my quarts of Busch?"

She called me an asshole and told me to get my own self to the unemployment office from now on. Which scared me a little. Joalene had done the financial statements for us. And it'd been three years since I'd been downtown. I didn't even go the river anymore, and the Mississippi's king. So I sure didn't want to go searching Waketon, on a bus, for some office of biggeties telling me all the things I should've done. It was a traumatic moment.

What I should've done is gotten up and said something, like told her, *Baby, all these years I know I've been bad, been a selfish swine, but in the future I'll be different. Promise. Soon as you can blink an eye, I'll be a new man.*

Didn't though. I couldn't. Because I tell you, I sure as hell didn't see any new man popping out of my gut. I did say, "Baby..." but then nothing. I clammed right up.

So she opened the door and let the frigid in, stepped out, turned around and told me, "I'm done caring for you, Sel. I can't do it anymore. I just can't." I didn't answer, and she waited a few seconds and then said, "Nothing? That's it?"

My head was still empty and my body cold from the winter coming in, so I just looked at her and shook my head. She spun away disgusted and slammed the door, and I leaned over the arm of the lounger, picked the old corded phone off the floor and set it on my belly and then called the grocery mart to have them deliver a few more quarts of Busch. But I heard Joalene's fan belts squealing in her old Malibu and then her tires screeching out of the driveway, and I got myself a hankering real strong for some chicken, which, because she'd grown up downwind of a chicken farm and couldn't stand the sight of it or the smell, even on my breath, I hadn't eaten since our first date in high school, three years before she'd moved in. So I ordered a roasted one, as large as they had, and mashed potatoes, and some slaw too, since I needed vegetables, and also a piece of chocolate cake. While the mart people were doing their calculating with the register, I looked out the window. The moon was gigantic and low. If I'd still been a farmhand, I'd've been out there harvesting into the night. But I wasn't. Just a guy staring at the moon that pretty much took the whole window. It was a beautiful thing, dammit, and it got me to thinking of Joalene when she wears her gray pants. Not that she's got an ass as big as a moon, but the pants are spotted, and she only wears them when she's digging in the garden, which is how we spent our first anniversary together—seeding watermelon and cucumbers and getting ourselves all dirty before we went to the fancy hotel, sudsed each other up in the whirlpool tub and then did what married people do on their first anniversary.

My eyes got foggy. And I don't mind admitting now that it was probably because of Joalene. No sense sitting and sulking all night though, so I said, "Dammit, Sel!" and punched my thigh—hard too, bruised myself—then I heaved myself out of the chair and put on my jacket, walked outside and stood and watched the moon. I stood so long I saw it move, which got me thinking about sunset and moonset and where Joalene was heading and if she saw the same moon I was seeing and at the same time? What would her watch say and what would mine if I had one, and would we be looking at the moon at two different times if there are two different watches?

The mart guy drove up and I paid and walked inside to the fridge and put the beer in. I found the forks and knives and napkins, got myself a plate and went to the lounger to eat. As I squatted to sit, I passed a little backside wind. And as I settled down I heard the chair squeak and smelled the thick cloud of gas from my insides—the putrid gas since Joalene had been forcing broccoli down my gullet. It was mixing with the spices from the steaming chicken, which should have watered my mouth, but nearly gagged me instead. Luckily, I only passed once, and since the chicken was still hot and steaming and still putting off its smell, I just had to sit quiet, breathe into my hand, and relax and let my bones settle and blood go while the nastiness squeezed its way out beneath the doors.

Once it had, I settled back and watched the clock circle and started calculating the minutes she'd been gone, and then the hours and the number of quarts I'd drunk that day, which wasn't many really—three, in fact, like every day. Then I took a bite of chicken and tasted that long-lost succulent flavor. I closed my eyes it was so good. Moist and falling off the bone but not overcooked, and with still-crispy skin that I tore off and let sit on my tongue while I looked out the window at the moon and wiped chicken juice from my chin. I took another bite and chewed slowly, trying to make it last. And I found myself doing what they call ruminating. I took another bite and chewed and ruminated some more, then another, and I kept on ruminating.

What happened, the thing that pretty much changed my world—not to say watching Joalene step out didn't— I'm not making light of that in any way; it's just not the same—but the thing that screwed with me bad was that two-thirds through the roaster, right after sucking the meat off a wing, I had something foreign and strange—an epiphany, a new thought. A decision.

What I decided was this: all we've been doing when we tell time, since we started telling time, is counting things. That's it. We've been counting. I wasn't sure what things the cavemen counted, but I'd seen on the old westerns some Indians talk about many moons ago, so I figured they counted moons. What other folks counted, though, I didn't know. I did know that I counted the number of times the clock went around and around and that every time the hours went around twice, I was supposed to put an X on the calendar and add one to the days. Simple. And I caught myself yelling towards the kitchen. "It's a count, baby. Time is a count." So I looked over and saw the counter clean and Joalene's apron hanging on the oven handle. The dish towels were all folded and her spices organized. I glanced to the bedroom. A lamp was still on. I mumbled, "Baby?" And then, "Joalene?" And I heard the sink drip, and the neighborhood cur bark, and the round clock tick and the water drip and the clock again tick, and tick, and tick, and tick.

2

DAY ONE

I woke up on the chair with the sun burning the frost off the window and shining on the walls in all sorts of yellows and blues and greens. My first thought was, of course, *what the hell time is it?* I looked at the two clocks—it was either 8:20 or 8:27. Early on both. The morning cars were rumbling up and down the road and the birds were tweeting. The cur dog was barking outside like normal, and like normal, its crack-skinny mistress was screeching at it to shut the hell up. I hated the noise in the morning, but I didn't care much that day because the coffee smell wasn't coming from the kitchen. I hated coffee too, but I found that I cared way too much about the missing smell.

So I pushed myself up and went to the bathroom, sat on the undersized seat and let everything out from both sides, then went into the kitchen for a glass of water, a leftover chicken wing and a slice of Joalene's homemade bread that she'd baked a few days before. After prepping myself a plate and opening my first of three quarts for the day, I headed back to the chair and recommenced to stare at the red numbers that were glaring at me back, screaming, *She's gone, fat boy. Gone and out and sipping a latte with some park-jogging Skip with hairless calves.*

"Prick."

That's what I said. Then I got to gnawing on the roasted wing, and I found myself ruminating again. And it wasn't about Joalene flipping her hair and showing her neck to some prima donna asshole with manicured fingernails. Not at all. I was thinking about Time.

It was the chicken. I don't know if chicken makes you smart like carrots do, but what I do know is that if the chicken's cold and the skin like rubber, although it tastes okay, the thoughts that come aren't as Big and Sudden and Clear as they are when the juice runs down your chin. But they do come.

See, I was thrown by the digital clock. It kept flipping over the numbers and telling me a minute's passed. But I didn't know how it knew. Now, I'm not a moron—I knew something was going on inside, telling the lights, *Okay, it's been a minute—flip.* But what was chunking along I didn't know. With the spinning clock, the second hand moves and you count for yourself every time it hits twelve. But the red numbers just flip.

So I decided to write my thoughts down, because my friend Herm used to write things down like that back when he was working through his bricking plans. But I hadn't tried. Then again, until that chicken, I hadn't had any Gigantic thoughts, which I knew that Time Is A Count thing was. Gigantic. I didn't know why. So I pushed myself up again and got myself a pen and pad of paper from Joalene's desk and sat back down.

Only writing wasn't really what I did too well, so I was only able to get *Time* down. *Count*—I wasn't sure if that was with an *ou* or *ow* or *k* or *c*, though I was pretty sure it was a *c*. But then there was *Count Dracula*, and I knew that was a *C* and that he was a whole different kind of *count*, so I wasn't sure.

I decided to tell people, because I'd finished the chicken and there wasn't another one, and I didn't want to lose my Time thoughts. I was worried. Really. So I set the phone on my belly, picked up the handset with the curly cord and called Herm.

Herm was on what he called a trial retirement, figuring that if his immigrant wife stopped working that he'd start career number two as a preacher or painter or something else that allowed for a flexible schedule—except for moving furniture and killing dogs. So now he's passing the time selling stuff online and house-husbanding and bowling and yapping with me.

Herm answered and said, "Hey Sel."

I said, "Hey Herm."

And he said, "Hey. Where you at?"

I said, "On the lounger. You?"

"On the computer. How's the gut? Churnin' good?"

It was our usual first-call-of-the-day greeting, which, besides our gastric states, usually included something about butt acne, our AAA baseball team the Blue Socks, how my checks were holding up, Herm's car and wife and, of course, Joalene. Which I tried to avoid.

"Not so bad," I said. Then, "Hey."

Herm said, "What?"

"I got a question."

"Don't call her."

"What?" It was more a yelp than a question, and I had to lunge to keep the phone from falling off.

"You okay, Sel?"

I ignored it and settled back. "She told you?"

"She told Susy Liu Anne. They're friends, you know."

"Only because of us they are."

"That's how they keep tabs, Sel. Befriend the friend's wife."

"But she shouldn't be blabbing already."

"That's why you shouldn't call her."

"I'm not calling her."

"That's right. Don't go crawlin'. Stand your ground."

"Dammit, Herm, I'm not crawling."

"Man up, Sel. Man up."

"Get off Joalene already."

"I'm just sayin'."

"Shut up."

"All right. All right."

Then, so I didn't lose my thoughts, which I was close to doing thanks to Herm, I asked, "So what's Time?"

"That's your question?"

"Yeah," I said. "What the hell is Time? Really, what is it? I know what wind is, kind of—a bunch of stuff blowing—and I know what weight is. Joalene won't—wouldn't—let me forget that. Hell no. But what is Time?"

"You didn't switch beers on me, did you? I'm tellin' you, don't be doin' that. Change is bad, Sel. And too much at once—it's real bad."

I hadn't changed beers, of course, given my sensitive gastric state. And I wasn't close to sitting up straight. I just wanted one answer to one stupid question. So I told him, "Just answer me, Herm. What's Time?"

"Crap," he said. "It's not the beers. You're thinkin' again, aren't ya?" He wasn't too happy about that fact. Neither was I, once I thought about it. "That's exactly what you're doin'."

"It just happened."

"Thinkin's bad, Sel. Worse than Change. Way worse. You know."

"I know." Not that my life had been chock-full of change, but there'd been one other time I'd settled in deep to thinking. Not long after the squashing of the Chihuahua, I'd been sitting on the lounger, warming myself with the sun through the window, when I saw a sun ray shining right through and sparkling on down till it passed in front of the TV. I got me to wondering why, if light was supposed to move so fast like they all say, why could I see it plain as day, just floating there. Then I realized it was dust I was seeing, and I started wondering why the dust was floating with no wind, and if it floated, why'd it land? Or did it start on the sill and take off? And if it did, how far'd it go? And how'd it get up on the top of the fridge? Did it start on the ceiling? So I set still, with my hand out, trying to see if I could see dust land. How long, I don't know. What I know is that before I saw even one speck settle down on my finger, Joalene'd walked in—I swear she'd been sneaking—and caught me staring at the air above my hand. That'd set her off on a six-week no-cooking, ass-chewing marathon. Wiped that thinking clean away. Like steel wool.

Herm, unfortunately for him, had lived a bunch of it with me. So he told me, "Maybe you should stop."

"Yeah," I said. "Maybe."

"But I'm not tellin' you to."

"Yeah."

"And it's not that you should stop calculatin' your checks and stuff. It's the other kind of thinkin'."

I sat there on the lounger, looking around at the soundless house. And I started going through all the old squabbles and rants and my blubbery gut and dust and all sorts of the things that had gotten Joalene all riled up. Thinking was one.

"You got a good life," I told Herm. "And a good wife." Susy Liu Anne, a nice little Mississippi Asian with an accent to make you melt. And sweet. Even though she'd befriended Joalene and they had their behind-the-back conversations, Herm was a lucky man. And he knew it.

The next thing he said was, "I'm a lucky man, Sel."

"You are," I told him. "Now, I got to go."

"Till after your quart, then."

"Yeah. After my quart."

I hung up, and he hung up, and I got a hankering to call someone else, just to shoot the shit about the Blue Socks or weather or traffic or something. But most people I knew had spit on their unemployment checks and gotten themselves another job or girlfriend or hobby. So the list was short. Down to one, actually. Which got me to thinking that maybe Herm and Joalene were right, maybe it'd be best to clear every last bit of Time and dust from my noggin. Settle it out with a good hard nap. So I stretched out the lounger and got my hands folded on my belly and my feet up. I closed my eyes, telling myself this was what I needed—a few hours of blissful rest. And then just when things were turning that fuzzy dream way, with everything sinking heavy, about a half second from nodding off, I got not just one epiphany, but three or four—*bam-bam-bam*—one right after the other.

3

AN EPIPHANIC FLOOD

The first new epiphany was that maybe it wasn't the chicken making me think. It was gone, and there I was having epiphanies. The second was that maybe Joalene and Herm were wrong and that thinking wasn't bad. Maybe it was the not thinking afterwards that was. Maybe that was way worse than the staring at dust and clocks and ruminating. So risking bad spelling and all, I wrote down my Gigantic epiphany, the one from the night before.

Time is a Count.

It was so big, I found myself staring at the words and smiling. But twenty seconds in I had another epiphany, which was complicated. I realized that I'm not a moron, but I'm not brilliant either, like I'm not some Gates or anything, so someone else had to have thought of this whole Time thing before.

But then maybe I am a moron, because I didn't think, *Hey, if someone else has already thought all this stuff up, why not just let them go on thinking about it, order yourself a pizza, and have another quart?* Like an idiot, I decided I had to start thinking for my own self, which should've put me in the bin right there. I almost went, too, got close to Loontown, as you'll see, all because of what I now call my Half Epiphany from Hell. If I hadn't had my Half Epiphany from Hell, I would've accepted, like normal, that those other thinkers know a heck of a lot more than me. Time being a count I would've chalked up as a bout with severe stupidity. New epiphany number two, about thinking being good, would have become obviously ignorant. Same with new epiphany number one, about it not being the chicken. I would have locked on hard to chicken being the source of my thinking woes and returned immediately to a life without fowl.

Everything would've been good—the Joalene part maybe not, but everything else, yes. Good. If only I hadn't've gotten my Half Epiphany from Hell and started down that twisted path into the tangled-up brambles of Time.

This is what it was: knowing that some people had probably been thinking about Time for a while and telling other folks and writing the stuff down, I realized that there had to be books out there about Time, good ones, that explain it all nice and clear and easy so as I could get back to my three quarts a day and napping.

It sounds simple, right? Like at most a half epiphany. Maybe even a quarter. But the repercussions of little things are big sometimes. The first repercussion of my Half Epiphany from Hell was that I decided to read some of those books. And I mean, really decided. Like, *Dammit, Sel, you're going to read. You're going to read until your eyes fall out.* Or close at least.

The problem with that was that I didn't read so well neither, about like my spelling. I could make my way through the baseball statistics, but a full article from the front page was—and I can admit it now—like heaving a hundred bags of manure onto a stake truck.

So I had to do some learning.

I pushed myself up and went over to Joalene's shelf and looked for some books that might help. This is what I read. I started with *A Wrinkle in Time*, since it wasn't so hard and wasn't long and had big print. It was pretty fun, really, if you like kid stories. Then, a week later, I moved on to *Life, the Universe, and Everything*, figuring that would have at least a few clues. But it didn't, particularly after I realized it was the third in a series and that I had no desire to read the first two about a hitchhiker. I got them off the shelf anyway, because I didn't want to skip anything, and since that's where the answer supposedly was—in the first one about the hitchhiker.

Waste of time. They're all muddled up and senseless and there's no way the universe can be like those books say. When I learned that the meaning of everything is "42," I nearly threw my quart. And it was half full, meaning I was really mad.

But I tell you, it got me to learning new words, like *repercussion* for one, and *epiphany* and some other words I was familiar with but not too sure of, like *cacophony* and *curmudgeon*, which is some cranky, old guy with a beard gnawing on about how bad the world is because he's picturing his wife leaning on the rail of a riverboat with some prissed-up, tie-wearing twit. But it's a cool word. The only bad thing—okay, one of the many bad things—was that every time I needed to look up a new word, I had to set my beer down, get up, walk over to Joalene's desk and leaf through her sixteen-thousand-page, super-deluxe *American Heritage* dictionary. And every time I touched her things, I got to wondering where she was and if she'd cut off her wavy hair and how I bet she'd look good with it short. Of course, she had a calendar hanging above her desk, so that got me to counting the days since I'd seen her, which were many. Twenty-six.

Finally, deciding that I wasn't going to stop looking up words no matter that it was like pricking my eye with a red-hot skewer, I got her twenty-pound dictionary and a couple of brown paper bags and cut and taped and covered the thing like I used to when I was a kid. Then I wrote on the outside in black magic marker, *Selraybob's Dictionary of Science*. There was a lot more inside than science, but I tell you, once I got the title on and set it beside the chair, the reading and learning got a bunch easier.

But before that, before I got into any more books, I had

another epiphany. It was: *I got me a dictionary, so it's got to have a definition of Time in it.* So I looked it up. There were twenty definitions about all sorts of crap, but the one I figured was what I wanted was the one I didn't understand for nothing.

A nonspatial continuum in which events occur in apparently irreversible succession from the past through the present to the future.

It made no sense at all, even after I looked up *continuum* and *irreversible* and *succession.* So I looked up *past.* It's a simple word, so the definition should be simple, right?

This is it:

The time before the present.

That helped none. If you don't know what *time* is, then how can you know what *past* is? And *count* wasn't mentioned anywhere. If the dictionary doesn't have *count* in it for time, then am I a moron or a genius? I'm not a genius, but the dictionary people should know what time is, and it shouldn't go round and round in circles. Should it?

I got myself all muddled and took a too-big gulp of my quart and finished it ten minutes earlier than normal, according to the clock with the red numbers.

What I noticed then was that I was aching to call Joalene, to jaw for a while about the grass and the moon that's getting big again—not near as big as the month before, but big enough to want to yell to the kitchen. But

Joalene wasn't there, I knew, so I sat some more and looked out the window.

Then I called Herm.

Herm answered, and he'd been having heartburn and I'd been having stomach grumbles something fierce that he figured had to be from missing Joalene but that I knew were from a severe lack of pepperoni, since I hadn't much felt like eating all that much for a while. Then we got to it. Herm asked me, "Still burnin' your days on that Time stuff?"

"I've been thinking on it some, if that's what you're asking."

"It ain't gonna matter none what you come up with, you know."

"It might matter some if I stopped."

"How?"

"I don't know. It just might." I couldn't explain. It was my gut.

"Sel…"

I interrupted him, because I knew what was coming—another lecture about thinking. "Herm," I said, "Let it go."

"All right then," he said. "Just don't forget."

"I haven't."

"Good. So, whatcha countin'?"

"The moon, I guess. The sun. That's a day, right? Around the sun makes a day."

"I think we're spinnin', Sel."

"I guess we are," I said. "But it's still a day. That's what matters."

Then Herm went all serious and said, "Okay, Sel, so answer me this. If a day is the earth spinnin' and the sun returnin', tell me—and *don't* you tell nobody else I asked this question, particularly the folks down at the Church of the 7th Day. All right?"

I told him all right, and promised and said, "Of course, Herm," like I'd be going out to church anytime soon, seeing as how my car was on blocks and Joalene was gone. So he said okay and asked me his secret question.

He said, "How does anyone know how many days it took God to create the earth if he created the earth on the first day and the heavens after, and on which day did he start the planets to movin', so as we could start countin' days?"

Then he hung up.

A minute later he called back.

"Don't tell no one, all right. No one."

"No one," I said.

"I don't even know why I'm blasphemin' the Lord like that."

"Didn't hear a thing from your mouth."

"Good."

Then he hung up again.

But the bastard left me zipper-down confused. So I opened my second quart and stared at it for a while and had another epiphany—it was a very epiphanic time for me, really. This one was that I always had three quarts a day—rain, sleet, or shine—so why couldn't I just count my quarts?

And that's what I started doing. I started ordering my pizza around the time I opened my third quart, went to bed well after I'd finished it and woke up a bit before my first quart. And I called Herm in between my first and my second. Three days running it was the same, without forcing it. So then, just to see how they matched, I started comparing my quarts to the clock, the round one, since that made more sense. What I found is that I pretty much finished my first quart around eleven and started my second around noon and my third around six. Within minutes every time. I'd always known I was regular with my beer—it's only that I used to look at the clock to see when to open my beer, and now I was opening my beer then looking at the clock. It's what they call a paradigm shift.

So then, figuring I was getting a grip on this Time Count thing, I started counting sips. Only, I kept losing track. I figured it was better to just look at the bottle and go with "right below the label" and "halfway" and "almost to the neck." Those, I decided, would be about as good as a clock, if nothing serious happened and I could keep myself regular.

Which got difficult.

After a week of counting my quarts, the full moon passed and my manhood died. I'd been manning up good for the month, because I didn't need her. No way. She could come to me. I'd do without the checks if I had to. I didn't need them or her—as long as I didn't tap the bank account much and we had the Discover Card and the account down at the mart, which was still going good, really, since I'd lost a bit of my food hankering, to tell you the truth.

But seeing that moon go small again, for the second time since she'd left, and the ice start to form on the window almost every night—well, that kind of shot my manhood in the neck. I leaned over and called Joalene's mobile, since she had one but I didn't. She didn't answer and I didn't leave a message, even though she could see from the caller ID how small my manhood had gotten. Oh well. That was nothing new.

What I needed to do, I decided, was to get out and away from that damn dripping faucet and the thought of a pink teddy I'd found in the back of the dresser that still smelled like cucumbers, which she used to like. And away from the phone, that I wanted to grab again. I shoved myself off the lounger, found my boots and jacket and put them on and headed out for a lap around the block.

I'd been outside to get a breath of air a couple times and a few others to let the mart guy in. But past the stoop, no. Not since the night of watching the full moon, which, if you recall, was the night Joalene left.

So I stopped outside the door. The cur dog was barking. Its mistress was screeching. The wind was blowing and my cheeks were already red with chill. I noticed myself shaking my head, wondering what the hell I was doing. A smart man would've turned and headed back inside.

Maybe it was my dictionary or that I'd read six books in the past month, which was six more than I'd read in the past four years. Or maybe it was noticing my manhood shrink even more in the cold. Whatever it was, I pulled up my hood, took a deep breath of winter and trudged out to the street.

I turned left, towards the cur dog. About ten steps from the mongrel's yard, the thing stopped barking and started staring up at me. When I reached the gate I stopped and looked down at its mangy mottled coat and weeping eyes. Of course I thought of Lexie, who was a lot smaller than the cur dog and much better groomed, but whenever Joalene was out, that little prissy dog would hop up on my lap, sit silently and let me scratch her chest. I almost reached through the bars to pet the cur the same way, but I got a vision of the squashed Chihuahua and figured I'd probably knock the fence in and break the cur's neck. So I headed on while the barking and screaming started again behind me.

I barely made it around the block, and couldn't drink for a half hour afterwards because of my breathing. Of course, then I had to chug my quart because of the pent-up thirst.

The second day was colder and harder. I even drank water I was so parched.

The third I walked the block in reverse and found myself sitting on the curb out front of the cur dog, waiting for the energy to trudge the last few houses home. The cur was quiet behind and looking at me, and I was wishing it was sitting at my side like a best friend, mangy and all, which it couldn't do, since it wasn't my dog anyway and wasn't even a friend. "All right," I told it. "I'm going." I pushed myself up. My knees cracked and ached.

The next morning my knees hurt worse, but I went anyway. I went left, like I'd done the first two laps, but only made it to the cur's fence and stopped there while it went silent and poked its nose through the rods. I figured if I didn't knock the fence into the cur dog, it'd figure out last second that I was a dog killer and snap off my fingers. And my knees hurt anyway. So I turned and headed back, walked into the house and opened a quart, sat on my lounger and looked at the clock. Not once did I think about Joalene. Not once. I just found myself staring at the red-number clock, mindless and stupefied, waiting for each *flip-flip*.

Somewhere along the way I got to seeing my "Time still to come"—me on the lounger, day after day, knees aching, watching the numbers flip and flip, not even counting because something else was counting for me.

Until Herm called and changed my future. Thank God for Herm.

4

Neglected Nostalgia

First thing Herm did was go on about the weekend's NASCAR race and how they're going two hundred miles per hour now and that it's too fast for the tracks, some of them, and that Earnhardt skidded into the wall and spun down across the track and into the grass. One other guy clipped his tail, but neither flipped so they're both okay. Only, Earnhardt was out of the race.

"That's what you need," Herm told me. "Some driving."

"You loaning me the Town Car?"

"I'm just sayin'."

"Yeah, you are."

"Better than burnin' your day countin'."

"If you say it is."

"That's what we used to do—isn't it?—back in school

when Joalene would hook up with my brother—go for a drive and drink a few quarts. Not talk science, Sel. No."

We'd skip science, actually, and go driving out to the bridge and sit and watch the river and drink beer.

Herm kept going. "If there's one thing an American can do when times are hard…"

"It's drive," I said. "I know."

"Damn straight!" He was getting himself worked up. But my car was in no shape for driving, so I asked him if he'd seen it lately.

He said, "I know what she looked like before you shut her down."

"I didn't shut her down. It broke down."

"And no wonder, the way you took care of her."

"I'm not a maintenance guy."

"So fix her up, and then let her go. A lotta people would love to have that car."

"I'm worse at fixing."

"She's a good car, Sel. Never done anything to you, except wear out while you was ignorin' her."

"Bastard," I called him.

Chipper as hell, he said, "I'll help."

"And what can you do?"

"Screw in a couple of bolts. Look stuff up on the computer. Buy refreshments. Whatever."

"We'll see."

"You got my number. Let me know."

"I'll let you know."

I hung up and sat there rubbing the arms of the lounger

and looking out the window at the empty branches. It'd been a long time since I'd driven even Joalene's car—months. I hadn't even gone for groceries; that's what delivery was for, and Joalene. It'd been even longer since I'd been under the hood of mine. For the past ten months it'd been on blocks without an alternator, battery or a starter. The whole system was mucked. It leaked gas, too, so I'd have to fix that. And the tires were probably flat, so I'd have to pump those up. I didn't even know about the brakes. Last I could remember they'd been squeaking. But I wasn't sure. Hell, I could barely picture the car in my head. All I could imagine was the white sheets full of dust I'd flung over a few months back.

So finally, after about two hours of mulling things over, I pushed myself off the lounger and went out to the garage where my car was—just to look. I lifted the front sheet and caught a glimpse of the red paint. Right off I got that sinking feeling you get when you see something you've missed but that you've left out in the garage alone for too damn long. "Come on, Sel," I told myself. "All right." I took a deep breath, pulled the other two sheets off and did a slow walk-around. Then I opened the garage to let the sun in.

She was still beautiful. Sleek and red. A Corvair. But not just any Corvair—they made lots of different styles. This was a 1964 Monza Convertible. Rear engine. Long, straight lines. Not curvy but not boxy. Lean. And misunderstood. Called dangerous back in the day, but no more dangerous than any other car of the time. Underappreciated.

I reached and touched her hood. "Sorry," I said. "I'm really sorry."

A few minutes later, without even sitting myself back on the lounger, I called Herm. "Get your mechanic pants."

"Oh, she'll be happy."

Herm came over that afternoon and the next few, and we drank our quarts and worked, and Herm read up on Corvair engines and wiring. He made runs to the auto parts store and ordered a few hoses online, and we tinkered and worked and cleaned and talked football and Blue Socks and the bad rap the Corvair got and maybe putting shoulder belts in and a stereo and how the river'd been freezing at the banks lately—anything so as not to bring up Joalene doing Pilates and yoga and tightening up her sexing muscles for her new lean, mean, screwing machine. It worked, until the fourth day, when politics came up and we knew we'd run our talk dry.

So while I was pressing my gut against the back fender, looking in at the spark plugs, Herm came out with, "How you gettin' her back?"

I answered him, "She can come to me when she wants."

"You're shittin' me?"

"I'm manning up."

Herm practically blew a gasket. "Sel," he said. "Shit. Mannin' up's good for a day, maybe two. Max, a week...*max*."

"It's been six."

"Exactly!"

"Thanks for waiting."

"You were still on your lounger, Sel." Herm put down his wrench and picked up his Bud to calm himself down. "I'm just sayin' you got to go after them, make them feel special and loved and all that. You can't wait. She's a strong woman, Sel. A strong one. And she'll be just fine on her own if you don't convince her she won't."

"I know." But it sucked to hear.

"So how you gonna do that?"

"Adjust the timing. Hand me the socket."

He did, and told me, "You should straighten that woman out."

"You should quit with your bossing."

"All right," he said. "All right."

We got to adjusting the timing, and I told Herm I wasn't going to think about her anymore. "Not now. *Now* we're fixing the car and *then* we're going for a drive. And we are not talking about Joalene."

Two days later we replaced the last plug, Herm pumped up the tires—using a compressor of course—and I poured in some gas.

"Ready?" he said.

I nodded. Slowly I opened the door. Herm was smiling. I smiled back.

"Go on," he said. "She's ready."

I lowered myself in, rubbed the steering wheel and gave the dash a little pat for luck. It was a few seconds before I finally put the key in and turned.

And she rumbled, nice and low and slow. And kept on rumbling.

"That's a good sound," Herm said.

I gave her a little gas, felt the vibration in the seat. "It sure is, Herm. It sure is. Let's drive."

5

SPEED

The sun was out. The frost had burned off. "Top down," Herm said. "Gotta start it off right." So as long as we could stand it, the top was going down.

I eased the Corvair out of the garage and down the driveway, tapping the brakes a few times, just getting a feel for her again. "This is how it should be, Sel." Herm stretched his arms high and leaned back. "Yes sir. This is it."

I turned left, drove past the watching cur dog and gave it a wave and a "Hey." The crack-skinny woman was in the yard and she gave me the inspector's glare all the way down the street, until Herm and I turned the corner and the barking started.

At the gas station Herm bought a couple of quarts and I filled the tank, and then we took her out to Route 143.

"Let her loose," Herm said. "Time to fly."

"You think she's ready?"

"Of course she's ready. She's been waiting for this. Come on. Let's go."

So I pressed on the gas and kept pressing and finally just opened her up. She was still fast. Flying down the road. I got to tell you that driving in my fast car, with my arm out the window and nothing but sky above—well, it's pretty sweet. I'd forgotten the exhilaration of acceleration, the pressure on the seat and the pull into the curves. There's not much better—not when Joalene's not there with her hand on my thigh and the Rams aren't playing the Steelers.

I checked the speedometer to see how she was really doing. The damn thing read zero. We were doing way better than zero. The wind was screaming around our necks and the car was shaking and the fields were going by like nothing, and before we knew it, I'd come on the dam at the river, which I knew was a long way. So we'd been doing more like eighty than zero.

That's when it all came back. What's time, and what's the speedometer really saying and how does it know? And what's speed if time is a count? Which it is, I decided again.

And my thoughts came out. "What's speed?" I asked Herm.

"Sel, you're thinkin'."

"Just answer the question."

He did. "Well then, shoot. Easy. Miles per hour."

"And that's how fast you're going?"

He leaned over to check the speedometer. "If it's

working, yep."

In the middle of the dam was a lookout. I pulled in and stopped, and we opened our quarts and sipped and looked out over the water. "So tell me," I said. "How do you figure it?"

"Well, you take the time you been drivin' and then count the number of miles you've gone and put the miles over the time, and there you got your speed. Miles per hour."

"Miles per hour," I repeated.

"Yep."

"So what's an hour?"

"Sixty minutes."

I felt my voice getting agitated. "And what then is a minute?"

"Sixty seconds."

"Sixty again. Sheez." It was like I was spitting at him when I said it.

"What's up, Sel?"

I took a swig and cursed and got out of the car. The discussion was getting me ticked off for some reason. I even yelled at Herm. "All you're doing is counting. It's all a goddamn count. You count one thing and you count another. Right?" He was still in the car and I was yelling across the open doorway. "Right, Herm? And you thought I was a moron for thinking those things." I took another swig, turned and looked out at the sun on the water, opened my shirt down to my gut and let the near freeze cool me down. Herm got out.

He said, "Never said you were a moron. Just said it was a waste of time."

"But it's a count, right? Time's a count."

That's when I had another epiphany. I mean, a Big one. I turned straight at Herm and said, "And speed's a count too. Just two counts. That's all it is. Two counts."

"I guess," he said.

"Well?"

"Huh," said Herm. And then "Huh" again, as if he was ruminating on it. "A count. Huh. Maybe."

I yelled, "Yeah! Two counts!"

"And you divide them, to get speed."

"Oh crap." I went quiet.

"What?"

"Math," I said.

"Oh shit," said Herm. Because he knew. I was actually better at reading than at math, and not because I didn't go to class, but because I didn't listen. I'd been on the football team. Left tackle. When you're left tackle for the Missouri state champs—not that our schools aren't kick-ass, because they are—it was only that if our quarterback, Reggie, Herm's brother, ever got himself hit from the backside, we would've been done for. I mean, he played for Notre Dame after school. He was good. And left tackle is the most important guy on the line when you got yourself a prima donna back there. It was Joalene who got me through school; she'd had a crush on Herm's brother.

"Well then, you can forget your Time talk. It ain't goin' nowhere for sure without math."

I cursed again.

"Whatcha gonna do?"

"Get a new speedometer."

"Good idea." And he whapped the hood in excitement.

"Easy now."

"Sorry," he said to me and then again to the car: "Sorry."

On the way back, Herm decided we needed a detour through town. "A quick cruise, show her the sights again." He gave the dash a quick rub. "It'll be good for her."

So we did, nice and slow, just cruising again, past the Windy Bar with its droopy flags and the Filmore Saloon, where we used to sit at the picnic tables and watch the girls dance. Herm had his arm hanging out over the door and smiled at the disbelieving passersby. One shouted, "Man, you guys must be freezing."

"Not in the hottest car on the planet!" Herm yelled back.

The guy shook his head like we were crazy. Herm grinned. "I missed our drives."

I was about to agree, but just as we turned the corner on Fifth, I saw at the end of the block, right outside the fancy new Mexican food joint, the unmistakable backside of Joalene. She had her hand reaching through the suit-sleeved arm of what I knew was that pamby-assed businessman with shaved calves. And they were walking towards the door, together. Like on a date. That bastard.

6

PLAN A

Herm was leaning out the window, smiling at whoever happened to notice him. I was focused ahead, at Joalene and Mr. Slick Hair.

And I was not going to chase. Never again. That was over.

I was manning up.

So I eased off the gas and rolled ahead at walking speed. Up at the corner, Mr. Slick put his hand on Joalene's lower back and opened the heavy wooden door while she flipped her hair and smiled at him in that squinty, flirty way.

I damn near ripped the steering wheel off. "Hold on," I told Herm, and jammed the gas pedal down.

Herm jerked back into his seat. "Hey!"

But within two seconds, before we'd reached the restaurant, Joalene and Touchy had disappeared into the shadowy booths of seduction.

"We're going clockwise." I screeched around three corners until we came back alongside the restaurant. We rumbled past nice and slow, and I looked in but couldn't see for the dark windows those Mexican joints put up. I wondered if she remembered the sound, since she used to like the old Corvair, particularly the rumble.

Herm had figured out what was up, and he asked me, "You goin' in?"

"One more time," I said, and headed around the block again.

I stopped at the restaurant, blocking traffic, and looked at the dark glass.

"You can't see nothin'" said Herm.

Another shaved-leg priss man and his bimbo girlfriend looked over and glared. "It's for hiding," I said. So with the Corvair still out of gear, I gunned it, nice and loud, thinking Joalene would hear that for sure, and maybe come running out and waving me down.

She didn't.

I grunted. "They put friggin' lime in their beer." And I popped the clutch and squealed down the road.

Herm got on me for not going in, and I got on myself even worse. Called myself all sorts of rotten words for sissying my drive-by. No matter the rumble of the car, if you can't go in and face your wife and her shaved-calf boyfriend, you sure as hell aren't manning up. So I cursed myself some more and hated on myself for two quarts and then finally decided, *Dammit, boy, you better get your ass in gear or just figure on settling yourself down till you rot through the lounger.*

I sat for about a quarter quart, wiggling around and checking out my lounger for squeaks. I spent a while longer examining the bottle, a few more sips checking out the tree, and a few more guessing how many steps it takes to get from the lounger to the fridge—about eight, I figured. It wasn't until I checked the hair on my calves that my mouth went sour and my eyes wet and I told myself to stand up, *Show yourself, you pamby-ass do-nothing*—Joalene's words almost exactly—that I shoved myself up, got a pad and pen from her desk and started making a list, right there, right at her desk. This is it:

> *Find her.*
> *Talk to her.*
> *Break the scrawny asshole's legs.*
> *Shower and shave every day.*
> *Clean up the pizza boxes.*
> *Tell her how much I miss her.*
> *Say the L word.*
> *Buy flowers.*
> *Buy lingerie.*
> *Buy a necklace.*

I stood looking down at it awhile, and ruminating on the *flowers*—dandelions, in particular—which she loved. But I didn't come to many conclusions or make any epiphanic decisions or anything, except that it was a list, and that I'd made it, and that it looked kind of like a plan. Which was big. Not epiphany Big, but I couldn't remember ever making a plan before, not even in high school. So since it was pretty much a plan, I decided to put in Steps, like add *Step 1* and *Step 2* and *Step whatever* in front of each little piece. I didn't reorder or rewrite or do any deep analysis; I just stuck the *Step*s in. At the end, though, for some reason, not that I was really thinking it was part of the plan, I added one more step:

Get a job.

That one got me kind of nervous, because I didn't want to go back to the silt collector or to the janitorial school, and I obviously wasn't moving furniture again. So I almost scratched it out. I couldn't do that either. That would've been like taking to the lounger with glue on my ass. Instead, I put *Step Infinity* in front of it, and then called Herm.

Susy Liu Anne answered. Her accent that I told you about is heavy Mississippi South, which is a bit out of place in Missouri. If I'm not prepared when she answers, I picture a cute little blonde, not Chinese eyes and black hair. She is sweet though, and not just with the voice. She asked me right out how I was doing and if there was anything I needed and if Herm had brought by the cookies, which he hadn't. I tried to fake it. I told her, "Oh, yeah, the cookies. Yeah. Um. Thanks." But I can't fake too well, particularly when I'm caught by surprise. She started cursing his backside raw, and even with the phone covered, I could tell she was on a tear. When she came back to me, though, she was all sweet and Southern and made double sure I didn't need anything. I told her, No thanks, but it was very nice of her to ask. Then she asked how the job search was going, and I asked, "Where's Joalene?"

She said, "I'll get Herm."

"No no no no. Tell me where she is."

As soft and dragged-out as she could, she said, "Oh, sweetie. I don't know."

"You mean you won't tell me."

"I would love to tell you, Sel, but I just can't. You'll work it out. She'll come when it's time."

"Is she working now?"

"She's got herself a new job, yes. But please don't ask."

"In town?"

"You know you're number two in my heart, Sel. You're dear. But don't."

So I said, "Okay. Secrets between women. Fine."

"I'm sorry, sweetheart."

"Can you get Herm?"

She yelled for Herm, and then nice as ever told me, "I think it's wonderful you fixed the car. Herm says it's running well."

I said, "Yeah, she's good."

"That's fantastic."

Herm took the phone and right away told me to wait, that he was going to the garage to talk. He came back on a minute later and started whispering. "Sel," he said. "Bad news and good news."

"No news," I said.

"He's married."

"Great," I said, as sour as I felt. "Thanks, Herm."

"With three kids."

"So Mr. Shaved Calves has spare sperm."

"You want the bad?"

"That was the good?"

"Yeah, well. The bad might not be so bad now that you heard the good."

"Sure." And I took a swig of beer.

"It's Reggie."

"Shit." I nearly threw the phone against my lounger—Herm's friggin' brother, the quarterback.

"She called him three times. And that was yesterday. And four times this morning."

"She's gone psycho."

"Yep. Didn't want to say it, though."

"Maybe this *is* the good."

"I told ya. He's up in Oregon, and if she's here like you say, then it's just a repeat. You can do what you did before, tell her how he's no good and womanizin' all over the place with girls under the bleachers. Because you know he's a high school coach now, so just because he's my brother and almost thirty don't mean he's not chasin' 'em under the bleachers."

My acorn started going haywire. I tried not to think about Joalene psycho-dialing. And it worked. Not one phone did I picture. Instead, I started remembering her in her cheerleading outfit, all rosy-cheeked and gawking at Reggie after the state championship with me all sweaty beside him thinking she liked me, and then learning she did, but that it wasn't the same. I should've manned up then, told her no thanks. But at seventeen and staring at the silkiest locks of wavy hair you'd ever seen and smelling her strawberry perfume floating up from her squeezed-in and puffed-out breasts, it's mighty difficult.

Since I'd gone quiet, Herm asked me, "You okay?"

"Yeah."

"Susy Liu Anne told me this. She said, if you're a girl, and if you got a crush on someone real bad and go through life without ever realizin' that crush, like settlin' down with the guy, sometimes you marry the guy right next to the perfect man. And you marry someone who's not so perfect but who treats you like an angel since the stud quarterback won't. And then, Sel, if she's always thinkin' that Mr. Stud is out there and still longin' for him and dreamin' about him during sex, then sometimes she'll freak out and go chasin'."

"She didn't dream about him."

"I'm not sayin' she did."

"Sure sounds like you are."

"It's just this. If it's a guy like my brother, a married man with three perfect kids in a pretty little Oregon town, then she'll come back chasin' you. That's what Susy Liu Anne says. It's a pre-midlife woman crisis."

"Yeah," I said. "Talk to you tomorrow." And I hung up, because while I was sitting on the lounger, staring at the quart on my lap, I got to realizing that sometimes, deep down, the guy knows all along. And when the guy knows all along that he's a substitute, he tries like mighty to prove he's not. He mows the lawn twice a week because she likes it short. He eats broccoli and Brussels sprouts. He even adopts a toy poodle and cleans the pee off the floor. But the guy never succeeds because his wife's still got someone else in her head. So he starts to spin a little off, buying gifts too often and apologizing too much, staying out too late one night and coming home early the next after losing another high-powered janitorial job. Nothing seems right because nothing is. Eventually, the guy starts thinking there's no use doing anything at all. May as well just take to his lounger and sit.

7

THE FIXERS

There I was, sitting on my lounger, staring at my half-finished quart and finally admitting to myself that from date one to the day she'd left, Joalene had been making do with a substitute, me, and that I'd up and quit on just about everything. It was a double dose of ugly.

Worse, too, those ugly thoughts had shoved Time right out of my acorn. I tried staring at the clocks, hoping I'd get some new epiphanies. No luck. The circular clock was like a movie projector looping through the time I'd caught Reggie and Joalene half-naked under the bleachers. And the red-number clock was like one of those funhouse mirrors that makes your gut look like an elephant.

Joyous.

My Busch had even gone flat.

So I sure didn't want to sit and ruminate on my rotten

realizations. But I didn't want to walk either, past all the neighbor folks mumbling, "There goes the second-string husband."

The only other thing I knew to do, good speedometer or no, was to drive. So that's what I did. I went out Route 3 and back across the river and back up into town, past the Mexican joint, around the Steak 'n Shake and through the drive-thru. I got a large chocolate shake, but no burger, and headed back through town, just to see who was where and what kinds of cars were parked outside the River Inn, Waketon's highfalutin hotel, where Joalene and I'd gotten morning-after anniversary massages and chocolate strawberries and where I half expected to see her beige Malibu again. Not that I was trying to look. I couldn't help it. I even got that drive-by urge, and I would've headed straight to her house if I'd've known where she lived, or where she worked now, or if her parents had moved back from Florida. Which I doubted, since they hated the cold. But I made a pass anyway by their old house.

The place was the same as in high school—tan with white shutters, an elm in the front yard, a fence in back and a lawn half-filled-in with grass that never would take. Her bedroom used to be around back, upstairs, and I thought about climbing the fence just to get a look at her old window. That had been a big step for me, once we'd started dating—from sitting in the car a couple houses down to sneaking around back while her folks were watching TV. I never even got caught. Not that I ever climbed all the way up, of course, but for a kid left-tackle-size, the one thing I could do, besides protect Reggie's blind side, was hide.

Which is kind of what I was doing driving around in the Corvair. The top was up, I had a hoodie on, and I'd driven an old Nova in high school. So even though I saw a few people I knew, since I didn't wave they pretty much missed me. I did refill the gas twice, for something to do, and bought a quart for something to do while I was driving. But I didn't open it right away. Didn't leave either. No reason to. I sat in the car in the parking lot outside the Rhodes 101 snazzy new convenience store and laid my quart in the passenger seat with my hand on top of it for comfort. It was a sunny day but still cold. A lot of flannel on the kids walking in—and boots and ski caps and parkas. I got the urge to break out my double-canvas jacket with the wool lining in between. It'd been folded for a couple years in one of my father's old footlockers out in the garage. It would smell, but I could hang it out a few days till it got fresher, unlike my beer, which was warming under my hand. So I backed out and turned the corner and wondered what time it was and if it was early to be drinking my quart, if I was to open it, or would opening it change time?

That's when I remembered the giant yellow clock that used to be on top of a building not three blocks down from Joalene's old house. I decided to take a right, and head back towards her old neighborhood to see if the clock was for something like a clock factory or repair shop. Instead, a Dunkin' Donuts was where I'd remembered the clock, so I drove around and around the neighborhood trying to figure if I'd remembered wrong or if they'd moved the clock, until finally I got a phone book and looked up 'clock' and got a whole long list of clock shops but not one near Joalene's old house. All the sudden, though, I got a hankering for Time, to see what other people thought, besides Herm. Like the clock fixers—they're all about Time. So I drove around and asked them. I said, "What's Time?" I did it politely, and not right off, because even though I figured they got that thing every so often, I'd learned from Herm and Joalene that Time's not a very good opening.

I got some insight back, kind of mixed. One guy said Time was what we're moving through, that it was how we measure change. Which was kind of like the continuum thing. So he'd probably read it in the dictionary. Another guy said it was the oscillation of the universe, and that we're in a big oscillation and Time just tells us where we are and if we're going out or in. But he didn't know which. This clock fixer with a Jesus sign said Time tells us how long it's been since Christ came and when Christ is coming back. So what I did was ask him Herm's question, about God creating the earth in seven days before there was a day. I figured if anyone would know, it was a Christ-loving clock fixer.

He knew, all right. Said it's easy. "First, God doesn't live like us. He's all-knowing and all over and he's got all those other stars he's creating, you know. And second, God had already created the day by the time he talked to Moses, and since God's all-knowing and exists out of Time, he knew exactly how long it had taken to create the earth and put it in terms Moses and the people of the time could understand. Which was days. See?"

I said, "Okay," and left and went to the next fixer.

At the next one was this dark-skinned guy who kind of looked Apache or something with a heavy forehead and practically black eyes. He told me the continuum story, and insisted that it was right, that anyone who'd spend their time, at this point in history, after all that's been proved, contemplating some half-crocked theory of Time was an idiot.

"Don't be an idiot," he said.

I left. But I told myself, *One more*, since that was a bad shop to end on. A few minutes later, after a few sips of my cool-but-not-cold quart, I stopped in a dingy shop with all of six clocks and one nicked-up repair counter with no one sitting behind it. I leaned over, and out from the curtain, which seemed a clock-shop requirement, came this long-haired, brooding guy who could've been twins with the name-calling prick from the last store. This guy was calm, but he had the kind of look that meant *Just because I look all calm don't mean I don't have a shotgun behind my back.*

I didn't ask him about Time or clocks or even if he had any clock-fixer relatives in town. I just said, "Nope. Wrong store," and took off.

Instead of pushing my luck, that the next one would be a terrorist cell, I decided, seeing as how I really hadn't been eating that much lately, except for a pizza late at night every once in a while—and even those didn't taste so good—that I needed real food. So I went back to the Steak 'n Shake and got myself a double burger and ate half the meat but all the tomato and then walked outside with a large Coke.

And right across the street, not fifty yards away, was Joalene's beige Malibu parked in front of this old brick building with two windows in front, each covered from the inside so that no light came out. Except for a neon sign stuck in the window well. It was a clock, and below the clock in bright red script was "Repair."

I swear, I was staring at fate—Time and Wife all tucked into a one-story brick building surrounded by metal warehouses and pavement.

I checked my shirt, which was yellow and now stained with burger grease. My waistband was unbuttoned for sitting-down comfort and my hair was unwashed, which I remembered was on my list, along with shaving, which I hadn't done either. So going over right then would've been torture, but staying away would've been a sin. A bad one. God will strike you down for staring his obvious plan in the eye and spitting on it.

An idea popped in, like an epiphany, except for the closest thing I'd had in a while was that substitution realization, which would've been nice to have missed. My new idea was that I'd do one thing at a time: first, sit and wait for Joalene to leave, then, second, go in. Which still would've been spitting on fate, just not with a loogie.

After another few minutes of ruminating on my future confrontation, I remembered the Mexican joint and Joalene's backside and my pamby-ass drive-by. So I called myself a few more nasty names, much nastier than even I can say, and hopped in the car, headed across and parked two spots down from the Malibu. I got out, took a breath, tucked my shirt in and smoothed it, pulled up my sagging pants and buttoned them up, brushed my hair back and finally walked in.

The bell jingled. I looked around. The place was as musty as a summertime trailer, and just a little bigger. The counter was in the middle, cutting the front from the back. Behind the counter glass were clocks, and on the walls were clocks and hanging from pegs were clocks all crammed together. Most didn't work, but some did, and the ones that did, all round ones it seemed, were *tick-tick*ing at all sorts of cacophonic times, as if not one was right.

I glanced around to see if Joalene was there. She wasn't. So I leaned over the counter thinking maybe she'd ducked down, and up popped this scrawny guy with scraggly hair and bulbous eyes and a pointy nose that would've jabbed my own eye out if I hadn't've dodged back.

He said, "Whoa. Didn't mean to scare you."

I said, "I'm good," and stepped back from the counter.

"Whatcha need?"

"You the only one here?"

He brushed his hair back, puffed out his sunken-in cheeks and yelled to the back. "Mochalita, sexy baby. You there?" I looked to the curtain where he was looking, cringing at the thought that Joalene had not only found another man but that she'd gone all the way around to a scrawny nerd-o-matic. He grinned at me all smug and waited. Then he looked back again at the curtain, shrugged when it didn't open. "Yep," he said. "Only one."

"Funny."

"Hey man. You asked."

"You sure no one's back there?"

"What—you're wife gone missing?"

I said, "No." And then, "Nope." And then I did a slow spin, scanning the clocks.

I stopped on this round-and-round one with spokes that lit with each tick—no hands. The guy said, "That's a nice clock there—a hybrid. Those are LEDs. Low energy. You can even turn off the tick if you want to, or make it change color, or play Mozart on the hour. If you're into that sort of thing."

"I'm not," I told him. "But what's Time?"

"What?"

I said, "Time. That's what you're tracking here, right? What is it?"

"Tracking?" He scrunched his face all frowny, gave me the suspicious scan, like I was a taxman.

"Yeah," I said. "Or counting."

"Counting?"

"With the clocks. Yeah."

"Why're you asking?"

"I've been thinking on it. That's all. I got some time and some clocks—two only, but they're different. So I've been thinking." His focus went to my gut, like he was boring in and measuring me. I told him, "Look. No big deal." And I started to leave.

That's when he said, "Ahhh," all nice and relaxed. "You're one of those home philosophizers, philosophizing on me."

"I'm just asking," I said.

"Come here."

So I headed back to the counter. Off to the side of the counter was a small round-and-round clock with black iron trim and a foggy glass cover. He pulled it towards him and started rubbing around the edge with his finger while he stared at me Buscemi-eyed and said, "You want the standard or the secret?"

I told him the standard first, and he went into the dictionary story of a continuum through which we move that tells us how we go and where we go in Time. "At least that's what the scientists say."

"And the dictionaries."

"But I know the truth." His grin flashed and faded and he leaned forward and stuck his eyes and nose and chin at me like bayonets, wiped his mouth and whispered, "It's a government conspiracy. How are they going to know where we are if they can't pin a time on us?" He nodded all solemn. "It started with Garfield—the president. That's why he was shot. There was a big Time revolt, and one of what they call the zealots figured it out and shot him." I nodded all solemn back to him and he went on. "It didn't help none. They're still watching us and tracking us. You be careful. Don't wear a watch." Which got me confused, until I realized there weren't any watches in the shop. Just clocks. And he noticed me noticing. "Uh-huh. Clocks only." I couldn't remember seeing a watch at the other shops, either. "You can go anywhere you want, but the clocks stay put."

"Okay," I said and started again to leave. "I'll come back if I want more information."

"Mondays, eleven to one. I'm here."

I stopped. "You're not the clock fixer?"

"I just clean 'em and watch the shop. He don't like to close for too long, and Monday's his lady-friend day. They take a while."

"Lady friend?" I asked.

"Not bad neither—from the backside. A little extra width, you know, and if she wasn't with an agent, I'd say she's okay. A good-looking woman."

"And they're eating lunch?"

It was a wishful question, I know—stupid. The shop watcher laughed and raised his hands, palms out, to show me how innocent he was. "Hey man. He's the Time fixer. I can't much say what they do."

"So when will they be back?"

"No telling. They finish when they finish."

"Great," I said.

After that I left and walked past Joalene's car and out to mine and drove across the street to Steak 'n Shake, parked in the back and walked in and bought myself a vanilla shake to settle my stomach, that was all the sudden bubbling up waves of sour bile.

Ten minutes after setting myself down in a spot with a view and sipping my shake, up drove a black sedan with dark windows. It turned into the clock shop and parked, and out from the passenger side stepped Joalene, all tall and sharp with her hair pulled up as if she was a model on the runway. Her backside didn't even look big. Almost slim in fact. Out of the other side came the Time fixer, as the shop watcher called him, and he was bald with glasses and round, like an old clock, except from all sides. He probably even looked round from the top, I figured.

They met at the front of the car and hugged—but they didn't kiss, which got me wondering if they were friends or customers and who was whose customer, which I didn't want to think about at all. But he was wearing a suit. Not even the Christ-loving fixer was wearing a suit. So Mr. Round was a pimp. But his suit was gray, not red and yellow pimp colors. He was her customer, then.

I belched up another hit of the sour, and lickety-split, she was in her car, out the back of the parking lot and into the alley. I thought of chasing her, but I didn't know where she was heading and figured I'd have to be screaming that Corvair around corners and up and down curbs and bumps and rocky roads to have half a shot. Instead, I stayed and watched the Buscemi-eyed watcher head out on his bicycle. I debated whether I should stroll across and beat the ass of the Time fixer or stroll across and strangle him until he told me what they'd been doing in his black sedan.

While I was debating, in walked Herm and Susy Liu Anne, all smiles and waving. And I saw a third option, which was to sit and listen to the petal-voiced interrogation by Susy Liu Anne. So I waved and put on a smile and stood up and said, "Hey Herm," and "Hey Susy Liu Anne," and waited for the Joalene questions to begin.

8

HAWKING

Herm went to the counter and ordered some food for them and a soda for me. Susy Liu Anne sat where I'd been, facing out, and I took a seat facing her—a glaring reminder of how lucky that son of a bitch Herm was. Her hair was silky black, her features slightly pointy and her figure straight out of a yoga magazine. And that's not including the cream-colored business blouse and dainty necklace.

She whipped out a box of mints, handed me one and said, "Sweetheart, it's so good to see you. It's been too long. You should come over soon. I'll have Herm cook."

I told her thanks and took the mint while she drawled out again how sorry she was to hear about Joalene's leaving, which didn't bother me much because it sounded more like music than pity. I told her thanks again, and she told me how nice the Corvair looked and how nice it was that

Herm and I had worked together. "It's so wonderful that you two are focused again."

"She needs a wax. But I'm planning on it."

What I was waiting for though, was the grilling, the "Why haven't you gotten a job?" and "She's a good woman—you don't deserve her," and "You're a fat slob, Selraybob. No wonder she left." Not that Susy Liu Anne had ever said those things to me—I was just expecting them. But then she reached back into her double-sized purse and pulled out a book. Self-help was the last thing I needed. And she didn't hand it to me right away, and all I could see was the corner. "I know you've been working really hard on that car, sweetie, and Herm told me how much you've been reading. So...well, I brought this book. It's an old copy of mine that I keep at work. It isn't pristine, but I thought you might enjoy browsing it."

I looked down at the book—*A Brief History of Time*—and then back up at Susy Liu Anne smiling as sweet as any Asian Southern girl could.

"It's physics," she said. "For you to keep. I've read it."

I almost went teary. Really. Because I'd been expecting a lecture and not support, and here I was with Herm's wife and she was giving me a book on Time, as if it weren't such a stupid idea, like I wasn't an idiot and wasting my time and Herm's time and everyone's. Because that's what I'd been thinking—until she handed me the book.

"You're an angel," I told her.

As if I'd given her a mindless thank you, she told me, "I hope you enjoy it."

"I will," I said, and yelled to Herm to order me a chicken sandwich, because I suddenly felt like eating.

I went home the happiest I'd been in years it seemed and sat down on the lounger, opened quart number two and started reading my gift.

It wasn't at all like those Universe books. It was hard. Who'd've thought that stringing together a bunch of words that I mostly knew already could confuse me a lot more than a bunch of words that I had to look up and figure out? Really, Mr. Hawking, the guy who wrote the book, got me muddled up good. About page three, I looked off to the side next to my *Dictionary of Science* and saw my plan.

> *Step 1: Find her.—I'd done that.*
> *Step 2: Talk to her.—Hadn't done that.*
> *Step 3: Break the scrawny asshole's legs.*

That one threw me, because he was a fat guy, fatter than me. Or at least rounder. He was definitely rounder—I had the height to balance it out. But I didn't really believe they were an item. They couldn't be. Still it went crawling through my acorn and festering good. Suddenly I was thinking he was either some prostitution client or he was running a whorehouse out of the clock shop. But either way, that meant that she was past Reggie. He was out of her head. She'd stopped calling. She was done. No more.

I went back to my plan. I got to figuring that if I couldn't do step number two until next Monday, I could break the guy's knees regardless—I knew where he worked.

Which pulled me to the list bottom, to the horrible one staring up at me.

Step Infinity: Get a job.

Right off I pictured me scraping the walls at the filtration plant down by the river and smelling the stench of silt and shit and rotting dead rats. I gagged. So I forced myself to think about something else. The only other thing that seemed to stick in my craw was Time, which prompted another epiphany, which were getting pretty tiring I tell you. Every one seemed to be getting harder and harder, and the latest one has been hard as all get out.

It was this: if I'm going to do what I'd planned to do, which was get Joalene back, it's not going to be from breaking the guy's knees; it's going to be from figuring out this Time thing and writing it down and becoming a professor or something over at the university. No flowers or jewelry. Maybe lingerie if I felt like it. No *L* word, and no damn *Get a Job.* Just:

Figure this Time thing out.

I felt good, excited. So I scribbled through Get a Job without feeling too guilty and opened Susy Liu Anne's book and started reading again.

And it still didn't make any sense.

First off, he doesn't start with Time or Time's history at

all. He starts with the universe and how all the scientists didn't know what was going on with it and how the sun worked and the moon worked and how the earth rotated and spun and tilted. It didn't fit with the title at all, and after slogging my way through that chapter I had to get myself up and wax the hood just to give my acorn a break.

But I slogged on, looking up words and ordering pizza and Q-tip cleaning the car whenever I got zipper-down confused and then coming back to the chair and reading some more, until after a week and a half I'd made my way through the whole two hundred pages, actually reading most of it. Two or three times.

What this Hawking guy did was talk about the universe, like I said, then about relativity, which kind of made sense but not really, then about the speed of light, and finally about Time, which he had to go backwards to get to. Which was just like the dictionaries with that Time-Past-Time loop.

See, I'm not a genius—I knew that—but I expected to see a paragraph, or a sentence at least, about Time being a count, which Mr. Hawking didn't mention at all. But because I'm not a genius and because everyone else says this guy Hawking is, I had to figure there was something else going on that I didn't see. So I wrote down some things, to see if there really was some genius stuff in there.

Here's my list.

—*There was a big bang.*
—*There was a singularity (which was just before the big*

bang, but I wrote it separately because it seemed important, and it's a pretty cool word if you listen to it).

—*The universe is expanding.*

—*The universe will probably shrink again. Maybe.*

—*There are many universes. Maybe.*

—*There are many theories, but no Theory of Everything.*

—*Time is an arrow.*

—*Time is the fourth dimension.*

I spent two days just on Time being an arrow and always moving forward, which Hawking proved by going backwards from a whole bunch of complicated things like thermodynamics, which I had to look up in my dictionary just to learn that it's all about heat and energy, which somehow make Time move forward into the fourth dimension of the space-time twilight zone. Which means I finally got the Corvair so sparkly that I had to take her out along the river.

Which is where I met the other woman.

9

FIXERS CAN BE FEMALE

I picked up my quart and drove out to the hills, but not too far, stopped off the road and started sipping. The sun was out but getting low and the air was cold and the beer warm from sitting in the car so long. I drank it anyway, at least most of it, saved the rest and headed back towards town.

On my way upriver I spotted on a bluff what I swear was that giant yellow clock that'd been by Joalene's. I could only see the top, not the hands, so I eased the Corvair down, turned off and headed up a winding road to the top of the bluff.

Sure as day, the clock was there, stuck on 5:30 just as I'd remembered. It was mounted on top of a clock shop, of course, but a big one. One story, but tall and modern, made of stone and glass and steel. And all by itself, like some fancy architect had built it to be his river-watching hideaway. I parked and walked in, still expecting the inside to be musty and for another brooding fixer to be glaring at me from behind a chipped-up counter. But I was very wrong.

First, the store matched the outside. It was clean and bright with silver clocks and brass clocks and gold clocks and steel clocks—all polished and shiny. At least a hundred of them, reflecting every move.

Second, and much more important, the fixer was a woman. And pretty, with just a couple lines on her face, black hair pulled around her ears, and this big smile and perky lips and those square glasses that models wear. Of course, I asked her, "You fix the clocks?" She smiled at me extra big, because she had a screwdriver in one hand and a tiny set of pliers in the other, and in the pliers was a tiny screw, and on the counter was a three-inch clock, open to the inside. I think my face went red, because it went hot. I laughed and told her, "Okay, I guess you do."

"I do," she said. And her voice had that depth that comes with age but not the age to go with the depth. It was just smooth.

I tried to act nonchalant, like I didn't think she was magazine pretty, but it had been eleven years since I'd been around a new woman who made me fidget. So I shuffled around in front of the counter, fiddling with my shirt, hoping some normal words would pop into my head.

"May I help you with something?" She grinned.

I looked down and grabbed the lip of the counter and she leaned across from her stool on the other side and gave me the cutest smirk I'd ever seen.

"Are you looking to buy a used one, or do you have something to repair?"

Make small talk, Sel. Or lie. You can do it. Tell her you want a gold one, with gold hands. Tall. But feminine. A gift for your niece.

"I'm looking for Time," I said.

She chuckled.

I said, "No, really. I'm just wondering what Time is. Or what you think it is. I asked some people, and I even read a book, but all the answers don't make much sense, so I was wondering what you thought it was, if you thought about it at all." Pamby-ass mambling explanation I realized I was giving, so I finished up with a quick, "I mean, do you wonder sometimes, in between fixing clocks?" and then shut myself up and tried to look away, but couldn't for too long because she seemed so sweet and gentle.

She was studying me though, and thinking, and it was feeling like time to go, so I started for the door. I got three steps without a damn answer, as if she'd gone deaf or mute or was playing with me. But then I heard, "It's a count."

"What?" I whirled around.

"Time is a way of counting events. Like ticks in a clock and the revolutions of these gears." I rushed back to the counter and banged my knee against it, giving her a startle and me a pain, but a short one because I wanted to reach across and hug her and kiss her cheek and maybe her lips and tell her, *Oh, baby. Oh baby oh baby oh baby.*

"Finally," I said. "Finally."

She laughed again, and her whole face laughed and her breasts rose, which were covered in a white frock, but I could see them getting wider and bigger and taller. She asked me what I meant by "Finally."

I stepped back, mumbled a couple *um*s, then told her, "That's what I've been saying. It's a count. Time is a count. Only no one cares, or believes. But you believe."

"Interesting. Because it was just a passing thought I had."

"Well you were thinking it's a count. Right? That's what you were thinking."

"That's what came to mind when you asked."

Her cheeks got pink, her mouth curled, and still her voice flowed. It was impossible to keep from bouncing on my toes and shifting around like a little kid. You know?—I was excited. I said, "Not some conspiracy or anything, right?"

She snickered. "You've been around the shops, I see."

"Okay, yeah. I have. A little. You know them?"

She kept smiling. "We're a tight group in a small town."

"But you said, count—about Time, I mean. You're the only one." I wanted to spill out about my professor plan. I wanted to tell her how I was going to write a famous theory and get a teaching job at the university and publish a bunch so as we—or I, at least, and she, if she wanted, not that I was really thinking that—could live on a ranch and raise horses.

She asked, "Are you a physicist?"

I stopped, went limp, and told her, "No."

"Astronomer?"

I shook my heavy head.

"What do you do?"

My excitement was gone, all of it. As alike as we were—not physically, since she was thin and pretty, but in our thoughts about Time we were—she was turning out like the rest of them, wanting to know what I did all day and why I didn't do more.

"Nothing," I answered. "I don't do anything."

"You're independently wealthy?"

I shook my head again.

"Hmm," she said. Dry and straight without a hint of curiosity. But still smiling.

"I fixed my car," I said. "A '64 Corvair. And I waxed it." I sounded like a high school dweeb. "And I guess I think about Time and read some, and I think some big words are pretty cool that I find in the dictionary. I've been looking up a lot of words lately."

I would've thrown myself out and called the police, because if I wasn't an overage high school dweeb, then I had to be a slow-minded stalker. That's what I would have thought—thrown off the short bus for pinching the girls.

"Well," she said. And even though she was still smiling, it had changed—less happy, straighter, kind of condescending, if I have the word right. "Good luck with your research."

"Yeah." My focus went to the grain in the metal front of the counter and on outlets on the floor and on my shoes—anywhere but up at her.

"It sounds like you're a busy man."

"I am." And I felt six years old and like a liar to boot.

"Well, I better get back to work. I've got a few clocks to fix before five."

I forced myself to take one last glance into her soft and pitying eyes, and I knew I needed a new plan. A real one. As soon as I got into the Corvair, it hit. And it shocked the hell out of me.

10

PLAN C

I got home and wrote my plan down.

1. Forget this Time shit.
2. Recalibrate my day to 5 quarts.
3. Really forget this Time shit and reading and the Fixers.
   Especially the Fixers.
4. Leave Waketon.

The first three weren't surprising, particularly number two. But what came out on number four—I'd thought maybe I would've put *Get a Job* again or *Clean Up* or *Exercise* or, at worst, *The Hell with the Whole Bleeping Female Sex*. But leaving—that was big.

It didn't sound so bad though, except for the money. I didn't have much. *We* had some, in a joint account, but I couldn't take it and run. Even though Joalene had. I got to thinking about that, how she'd taken off and hidden and was lunching with the round man. So I called Herm. I told him about my action plan. He told me Hawaii.

"If you're goin' to go, you may as well go to sun."

"Isn't that quitting?" I asked.

"Of course it's quittin'. But so what? Get out."

"It doesn't seem right."

"Get a tan. Go. And you know what, forget Joalene. She's still pinin' over a high school crush."

"I guess I'm doing the same."

"But yours just walked out on you."

I leaned back and took a sip of my quart, not sure what number, maybe sip four, and told Herm, "I met a girl."

Herm yelled into the phone, "Well shit, Sel! Take *her* with you!"

"But I was a dweeb again."

Then he started cursing at me. Not in the mean way, but in the way that's wishing I'd do better for myself. The friend way. After he was done, after he'd apologized and I'd told him it was okay, that he was right, we hung up and I sat awhile thinking about bikinis on the beach and the pretty clock fixer and Joalene. That thought got me up and I went to the garage and started a load of laundry, came back into the bedroom, pulled out my suitcase and looked around at all our stuff—the stereo and my father's Jethro Tull LPs and the phone and lamp and bed and my clothes. There wasn't much there I really needed. Not out front either. I didn't need plates or silverware or spices. Wasn't taking the TV—it was old and needed a special converter anyway. I just needed little stuff really, like the tent in case I got in a real bind, and a pillow and some aspirin and a cooler for snack food. But not much else but clothes—and the Corvair's much roomier than people think, really.

But sitting by the lounger on my beer table was the *Dictionary of Science* and my notes, and I got to thinking I was quitting. I was letting it all go and letting everyone win, and I was quitting.

You'll never amount to more than a worm on a pile of mole scat.

Okay, Joalene, I thought. *As if it matters anymore.*

And I went back to the garage to check my laundry.

I spent the next two days cleaning up the place so it wasn't ratty for whoever it was that was going to come next, maybe Joalene. And I did more laundry and folded my clothes, and when I'd get fed up with the organizing I'd sit down and reread parts of the Time book, confirming to myself that Hawking was a loon and that I wasn't a moron. Then I'd get over-read and go out to the car to check the fan belts and spark plugs to make sure she was working all right. It was a very productive period now that I think about it. Only, after sweating over the Corvair and rubbing her down and cleaning her up inside and out, I realized I wasn't leaving her. So that left out shipping off to Hawaii. I started thinking maybe California instead, because I knew a few people there, like my friend Plato—yes, that's what his parents named him, but I'm not sure it fits. I thought also about Florida and hooking myself up to some yacht charter, which I'd seen on TV, and bartending myself to the Caribbean and back. It didn't sound so bad. And that's finally what I decided would be it—Miami.

So I drove to the bank to check our balance, which was bigger than I'd remembered, a lot bigger, like a prostitute's amount bigger. A grand. Practically double what we'd started with.

I felt sick.

I hopped in the car and drove around telling myself, *She's not prostituting herself. She's not. No. She wouldn't get naked with some round clock-fixer guy for a couple hundred dollars a pop. She just wouldn't do that.*

Or would she?

No!

Whore.

So my little run to the bank became a search for the hips I used to love, and for the moon man with a big wad of cash. I drove past the Steak 'n Shake, behind the clock shop and up and down practically every street in the city. At lunch I parked in the downtown square and watched the people go by. I even walked into the Mexican joint and paid for a double-sized beer—no lime—expecting at any minute for Joalene to strut in with some college punk. After another beer, I found a pay phone around the corner and called Herm and Susy Liu Anne and practically begged for information. But Susy Liu Anne kept to the woman code—not a word about Joalene's job or apartment or new phone number. She just told me how good a guy I was and that there was nothing to worry about, that Joalene wasn't prostituting herself.

Right.

Three days I spent driving the town and scanning the streets before finally I got so worn out from being ticked off that my hunger kicked back in and the craving for another roasted chicken. So I headed to the minimart—the last place in Waketon I expected for Joalene to pop back up.

She did, of course, and two more times that week.

11

The Meaning of Lasagna

While I was walking up the sidewalk, about half a block away from succulent, mood-enhancing, epiphany-creating roasted chicken, up drove this shiny red Camaro. It rumbled up and parked three cars down. And out stepped Joalene. She was wearing a hip-hugging skirt and a shiny cream blouse that was open low, showing off her smooth and tan neck and a bright gold necklace. She saw me and said, "Hey Sel."

I wasn't even sure I could muster my voice. With my anger drained away and my stomach churning, all I wanted to do was duck into the mart. But there were the chickens inside, and even though I hadn't been in the mart since before I'd gotten the car going, I figured with the chickens roasting and dripping with spices and oil and chicken juice, making your mouth water just being in the same room—I figured that the smell, as good as it is to me, would stick to my shirt. And if I came back out again and Joalene was there still, she'd gag and run. Which shouldn't have mattered, I know. But it did. Too much. And I hated that it did, and that my throat felt tight and my tongue swollen. I may as well have dug my head into the mole scat and smelled my own weakness. *Weak little worm,* I called myself. *Man up. Man up, Selraybob. Man up.*

I pushed out a soft little, "Hey Joalene."

Pathetic.

She walked around the Camaro to the sidewalk and asked me how I was doing. I told her,

"I'm good."

Still pathetic. Maybe even more pathetic.

And as she was checking out my elastic-waist pants and T-shirt, my thoughts flashed to scowls and scorn and pointed fingers telling me how much more I could do. More. I could always do more. But never enough. That's how it is when you're the replacement for perfection. And just as I'd expected, she asked me, "You working?"

I answered her: "Nope."

She wasn't even disappointed—she'd been expecting it. I could tell by her smug little smile. Which got my anger turning from the in to the out, at her. I said, "You got a new job, I hear."

"I did. It's something different."

"Different how?" You're screwing now, is how—that's what I was thinking. Finally sharing herself with a man. One who has money.

"Just different. An office. Everyone's got a degree around me. Even the receptionist."

"Lucky you." Deceitful woman.

"I wasn't saying anything about you, Sel. It's different, that's all."

"Right."

I started up the street, and she yelled. "Dammit, Sel!"

"What is it now?"

I think she wanted to slap me. "I wasn't throwing it at you."

"Yeah, well. You used a shotgun, then."

"No. I didn't mean to. It's just that it's not like the warehouse. It's different to be around different people and actually work with them."

"I'm sure it is."

"It's a good change, Sel."

"Change is good," I said. "I'm glad you're out of the warehouse."

We stood for a second, a couple yards apart, neither of us speaking. Joalene fidgeted around a bit, then reached into her purse and checked her phone for messages. From one of her special, degreed colleagues, I figured. For whom she'd probably spread her legs. On the hood of the Camaro. Joalene shrugged, closed the phone—no message. "Well, then…," she said.

"So, where are you working?" I was glaring good.

She paused and shifted her hips out but didn't rush off.

I waited.

She said, "I can't…"

"Bullshit."

She yelled, "*Sel!*"

I yelled back, *"Where the hell'd the money come from?"*

"A bank!"

"No shit. Of course a bank."

"That's where I work, Sel. A bank. All right? I work at a bank." She turned away and shook her head so that her hair went swooshing slowly across the back of her neck. And in this low, mean whisper, she told me, "And don't even ask me what bank it is. All right? Just leave it."

"So why'd you use our account, Miss Banker?"

She spun back around and snapped: "Because I didn't think you'd make it to the unemployment office."

"I don't want anyone else's money."

"You had no problem when I handled it."

"Well I don't want yours," I said. "Take it out."

"Fine."

That was the end of meeting one. Ruined my appetite.

The next day, I had the Corvair out again, putting too many miles on her, when the rain started and the temperature dropped. The heat in the Corvair works, but it's no Rolls when it comes to comfort. So I ducked into a coffee place for a hot chocolate. They must have had all pots brewing at the same time, because the coffee smell was crazy. Instantly I pictured myself in bed, with Joalene in the shower and the coffee wafting in from the kitchen. It only figured she'd get in line behind me.

First thing she said was, "Sorry about yesterday."

I said, "Me too."

"You know, it's just…"

"Yeah."

I started glancing around, and she started glancing and rocking from foot to foot. A codger said, "Excuse me," and stepped between us on his way out. As soon as he was out, we resumed our glancing around. I had to say something. Something manly, I told myself.

So I said, "I got the car running."

"I heard."

"Took her out on 143 the other day with Herm, to do some…well, just to see how she ran."

"That must've taken a lot of work."

And there I was, a kid again, fourth grade this time, getting a compliment I didn't want but one that made me feel good anyway, and pissed off that it did.

"Herm helped," I said.

"He's a good friend."

Then I stepped towards her. I don't know why exactly, or what was screaming through me, but I got one step away, and I saw the makeup flaking from her chin and I smelled her perfume and remembered tasting strawberries on her breasts, the ones pushed up beneath the shiny new necklace. So I gave her as svelte a smile as I could, and I asked her, "You want to go for a ride?"

She gave me another vertical review. "Did you lose weight?"

"Don't know," I told her. "I don't weigh myself. And with these waistbands"—which I tugged on as if she hadn't seen them—"you never can tell how your waist is anyway. But thank you."

"You have been eating, though, haven't you?"

"Some."

"From the mart?"

"Mostly," I said. And then, back to the Corvair: "So...you want to go?"

"I can't."

"She's running real good."

"Sel...I can't."

"Your Camaro's nicer. Newer. I know."

"It's all right. When it's clean. It's already dirty."

She walked up to the counter and ordered a latte. I eased beside her and told her, "You know, I did some cleaning."

She glanced at me sideways. "Besides the car?" she said.

I said, "The house. I even scrubbed the floor."

"No?" And there was true disbelief. "With what?"

"The brush in the garage and some soap under the sink"...that had taken me twenty minutes to find.

"Now you'll tell me you shut that dog up down the street."

It took me a second to answer, because after years of crossing streets to avoid dogs, all dogs, particularly the small ones, and looking like a pamby-ass coward to every witness, I didn't want to tell Joalene I'd gotten the urge to lean over a flimsy old fence and pet one. She took my hesitation as a sign of the dog-hating murderous streak she swore I had. But at least she made a joke of it, as she'd started doing the last couple of years.

"You didn't feed it the Clorox, did you?"

I went extra hearty and bellowed, "No no. It's still got a healthy set of lungs."

Joalene laughed, which surprised her, and me too. And that's when I remembered what had really gotten me in the first place—her laugh. Her whole body moved. Even with the smallest giggle, everything got to shaking, as if her fingers felt the laughter, so if she touched you while she was laughing, you felt her joy.. It made you quiver. She said, "And Madame Screamer's probably going right back at her."

"They're two great conversationalists."

"Conversationalists?"

"Yeah."

"You've been reading."

"Some."

"That means you could make it through a cookbook, if I was to find one for you."

I laughed back. "Cars and kitchens don't mix," I told her.

"You're right. Don't rush it." Even though the jokes were about me, it was fun. She was wiggling and smiling and I was smiling and getting that warm feeling even without the coffee.

Until her coffee did come and her smile turned forced and she left.

The day after that, I got a call from Susy Liu Anne. She

told me I had a gift waiting for me. I asked her, "Does it relate to women?"

"To one."

"Which one?"

"Sweetie, you know which one."

"Is it a jump rope?" Because that's the kind of gift I'd expect from Joalene.

"Lasagna."

"No. Really?"

"A full pan, I believe."

"Cool." Joalene did make good lasagna, and right off I got a hankering for home-cooked, familiar, spicy, triple-cheese-layered pasta. I'd even heat the oven if I had to.

"I'll drop it off in the morning. Are you going to be around?"

"How about tonight?"

"I don't have it yet, sweetheart. Wait for the morning."

That afternoon, the lasagna anticipation was getting me so twitchy that even a quart didn't help, so I drove downtown, to see what the buildings looked like. I parked and walked and looked up at the new, all-glass bank building that would've been nothing for St. Louis but was a skyscraper for Waketon. Right after I'd sat on one of those new metal benches and stretched my sweatshirt to tuck it under my butt for warmth, Joalene came up behind me, and startled me. "Hey, what are you doing here?" she said.

I jumped up. "Watching the clouds," I said, because they did reflect off the glass, and they had been skimming across the sky pretty good. "It's like they're chasing each other."

"They do that."

"And what have you been doing? Besides work, I mean."
She was wearing heels, but not too tall, and another
backside-hugging skirt with a jacket to match and a
shimmery little shirt. Very professional. And very pretty.

She had a coffee in one hand and held it up for me.
"Coffee break," she said.

I should've figured she wasn't alone, but I wasn't
prepared, again—as if I was ever prepared—for what sidled
up all smooth and cocky beside her. Mr. goddamn Priss
Man. His hair was short and parted to the side nice and
neat. His glasses were the rimless trendy ones. His suit coat
was tailored, and it fit him way too well. I could guarantee
you that under his pressed pants his calves were oiled
smooth.

And first thing he did was stick his hand out, give me a
big ole friendly grin, and introduce himself. "Simon," he
said.

Just what I wanted, a pleasant greeting with the new
Reggie. I shook anyway and said, "Hi."

Joalene was far from wiggling joy, and she went formal
and introduced me.

"Selraybob," she said.

Simon said, "Ah, yes. Selraybob. The Ex. Finally a face
to a name."

"The Ex?" I asked Joalene. "Ex?"

And to Simon she said, "We're separated, actually."

"I see." He nodded and smiled and checked his watch.

"I've got to head back." Again he told me it was nice to meet me, and to Joalene: "I'll see you at the meeting."

"I'll be right there."

Simon left. I said again, "Ex?" And I noticed her bare ring finger. "Ah shit, Joalene."

"I don't wear it at the new job. It's better that way."

"So all the priss boys with three degrees can hit on you."

"You haven't worked in two years, Sel."

"And what about Reggie?"

That brought the scowl and glare. "Who said anything about Reggie?"

"You've been calling him."

"You have no idea what you're talking about."

"How many times have you called?"

"This isn't about Reggie."

"About your priss man, then. He was a quarterback, too, wasn't he?"

"That doesn't matter."

A few college kids walked by and a few more businesspeople out on break—jeans and cords and suits and me in my sweats. "It's always mattered," I said.

"Sel, this is not about quarterbacks. Or Simon. Or Reggie. Not even you. I needed time to think. That's all. I just needed to sort things out."

All the sudden I spit my words at her. "Time to think— bullshit! I'll tell you what I've been thinking about—Time. That's exactly what I've been thinking about since the second you walked out."

"Aww, Sel."

"Don't 'Aww, Sel,' me."

"So you're still on the clocks?"

"Not clocks—Time. I'm still on Time. Right on it, baby. Been reading about it, thinking about it. Time, Joalene. Time all the time. I got a new theory of Speed, in fact."

As ruffled up as I was, what got to me was that Joalene wasn't mad at all. Her shoulders had sunk, and her voice with them. "It's a dead end, Sel." It was as if I'd made another dead-dog blunder at another early-morning job. And I hated seeing her droopy. It sent me even lower.

All I got out was, "Maybe." Because she should've been mad, dammit.

"You're wasting your time...no no. I'm sorry."

"I don't know. But maybe, Joalene...just maybe I am *not* wasting my time. Maybe there's something to it."

"Sel, smarter people than you spend their lives thinking about that stuff."

"Yeah, I know. But..."

"It's their job, Sel. They're experts. You got to quit with these fantastic ideas and start living in this world already."

I didn't answer.

"You're wasting your life, Sel. And it's sad." Then she reached into her purse and pulled out her super-smart smartphone and read something and told me, "I've got to go. I'm sorry."

"Sure."

"They're waiting for me."

"I'm sure they are," I said. "I'm glad things are going so

good for you."

And that's when Joalene answered, "They are," and gave me the same smile that I'd been faking, as if big things were happening for me, as if Time was changing my life, which it wasn't, which meant she was faking. "I've got to go," she said. Then she scurried after Simon, turned a corner at an old stone building and was gone.

I sat on my lounger the next morning with a slab of lasagna in front of me and a quart on the beer table beside me. As I looked at the mountainous layers of pasta and cheese I began wondering. Was she feeling guilty? Did she make another pan for the moon-man clock-fixer? Was she screwing that back-waxing prep? Did she like me again? Why didn't she get mad?

I took a bite. Not as good as the first go at the roasted chicken, but tasty. And different completely—one food was long lost and forbidden, and the other the last real meal I'd eaten with Joalene. Maybe that's what she wanted me to remember, because it'd been a good dinner, just three days before she left—both of us eating on our laps, sopping up the sauce with garlic bread and talking about Herm and Susy Liu Anne and maybe getting another dog, if I could handle it. It made me miss it all. So much so that I snarfed the slice down and shoved myself out of the lounger to head to the kitchen for another round. But then my stomach gurgled and a bubble of gas got lodged just above my stomach. And it seemed to swell. I felt like a swollen, blubbery sea lion. Add in a mound of pasta and cheese and

I was one bite from exploding.

Then I got it—she's fattening me back up so she can pity her triple-sized man sitting on his lounger while she's out chasing the quarterbacks and slicked-up priss-boys with slick phones and slicked-back hair. The type she'd always wanted. So I put the plate down, put my shoes on and headed for the front door, for a walk, a long one, all the way back to my football roots.

12

FOOTBALL

First stop on my back-tracking journey was at the cur dog. I stood by the fence looking down at it and it looking up at me, waiting to see what I was going to do. I decided to risk it. Making sure I wasn't leaning on the fence, I lowered my arm, opened my palm and spread it across the iron bars. The dog sniffed. I pressed my other palm against the gate, which was extra risky to my balance. It sniffed that one, backed away as if thinking, then turned, leaned full body weight into the fence, stretched its neck out and looked up at me. "Okay," I said, and reached my fingers through the bars and gave it a little neck scratch. It's fur was rough and dirty and its skin beneath flaky. I pulled my hand back, and the cur dog spun around lickety-split, leaned its other side into the fence and gave me a weepy-eyed look as if it hadn't been scratched in years, and had forgotten what it felt like, and the memory made it sad to the point that it was willing to beg for more. So I reached over the gate and scratched its raspy back. I know I saw at least four cars pass before I left, and cars don't pass that much during the afternoon, so it was a while before I pulled my hands up, wiped them on my pants and told the dog, "See you later." It wasn't till I was half a block down, near out of sight, that the dog started barking again.

I ended up a mile from home, down by the park—the farthest I'd ever walked. Three kids were playing football, and I stopped and watched them and thought of Joalene in the stands and Reggie bombing it downfield and patting my helmet afterwards and telling me, "Good job, Sel. I'd die without you." He wouldn't've died of course, but I was a pretty good tackle, and he would've taken a few extra knocks, and we might not have won state if I'd been guard, or if my dad would've moved after losing his job.

The park kids were pretty good too. At least two of them. A chunky guy was hiking it and a tall kid with long arms was playing quarterback and a little fast kid was streaking out for the catch. I don't know what got me to do it, but I walked over while they were huddled and said hey, and asked them if they played on the team. I figured junior high, or the freshman league, unless the quarterback was good enough to move up. But it was the chunky one I was asking. He's the one who shook his head no. The tall one answered, "Yeah. We did. Season's over though."

The short one ran back with the ball. "You talking about the team? We were bad."

'How's your line?" I asked.

"Worse," they said together.

"I got sacked a lot," said the quarterback.

"You got to have a good line," I told them. "It all starts up front."

They said, "Yeah." But the chunky kid, soft in the middle but not so dumpy he couldn't do something with football if he really wanted—he hardly even looked at me.

So directly to him I said, "Hey. You on the team?"

He shook his head.

"You ever want to be?"

"I don't know." And he tucked his chin down and shoulders up. "Maybe."

I'd been thinking the same about a lot of things besides football—all muddled up. But to the kid I said, "You're out here now, aren't you?"

"They needed a hiker," he said.

The tall and spindly quarterback said, "He's a faller."

"My balance isn't so good. I have to hike from the side." Instead of between his legs, like he would on a team.

I told him, "That just means you got to get low."

So the sprinter tossing the ball up and down asked me, "You ever play? You don't look like it."

"Yeah," I said. "I was a tackle."

"For the Rams?"

They were thinking the St. Louis Rams, and it got me laughing. "No," I said. "Just high school."

"That's too bad."

"We won state. Only Waketon team to win state, ever."

"Like twenty years ago!"

"Eleven."

"You still old."

That was the reaction I should have expected from the little fast twit thinking he's going all-star in a season.

Then the quarterback said, "You know, we were last. South Middle. One and eight."

"You got a good arm," I told him. "And he's fast." I nodded to the little guy.

"We're good." That was the little guy, pointing to himself and the quarterback.

The quarterback was more modest. "We're all right. But the team's bad."

"Maybe what you need is a good left tackle to protect your blind side." I was pointing my chin at the chunky boy. "Left tackles get paid almost as much as quarterbacks."

"I told you, Carl," said the quarterback. "You should practice. You're big."

"It's fat," answered the chunky kid.

I said, "You work a little, you can build the muscle underneath."

"You need to start lifting weights, Carl."

"Yeah. Come on."

"No," I said.

The quarterback was darn near as tall as I was, and he was to one side and the speedster was to the other, and they told me simultaneously, "You're crazy. He's gotta lift."

Punk kids. So I asked Carl, the hiker, "You like lifting weights?"

He shook his head.

"Because everyone's watching you, right? And they all think you should be super strong since you're big."

"I guess," he said.

"I know," I said. "That's how I was." Big, with a gut full of burgers and fried chicken and fried everything. But no muscle.

"Still are," said the quick one, laughing.

"There's plenty of muscle underneath."

"Yeah. Sure there is."

I leaned his way. "You want to find out?"

The quick kid tossed the ball to his side and ran for it. I continued with Carl. "Okay. I'll give you two ideas. If you want to use them, use them. If not, no problem."

They all stopped and waited.

I squatted as low as I could get, which for years I couldn't do very well on account of my pants being tight, even with the elastic. But they weren't that tight anymore, and I could get darn near to a full-blown squat. It shocked the hell out of me that I could bend them that far without pain streaking up my legs. Just an ache. But that was good, particularly after my walking. And I had to make it look good for Carl anyway. "You get like this," I said, with my arms out and my palms forward. Then I started shuffling around with my butt sticking out. "And you push yourself up and around from side to side."

The cool kids laughed. "You ain't doing that at school."

"That's for home," I told them. I rubbed my thighs, which were starting to burn and which I knew would be sore. "It's not so easy."

The chunky boy tried it and got about a quarter bend before he started losing balance. So I told him it would come, that I used to be stiff and fall over too, but that the squatting helped. "You just got to line up your knees with your feet so you don't get hurt. That's super important." At least that's what one of Joalene's yoga shows said to do. "Stretching's good too. It'll help you bend."

"What else?" he asked.

"Walk up stairs, with something heavy on if you can— you have stairs?"

"Yeah."

"Walk up as much as you can, two at a time, and do it faster and faster, and next thing you know, you'll be strong in the legs, powerful, which is what matters most to a tackle—power to stand firm and push off."

The football lesson made me remember knocking linebackers on their asses and defensive ends on their asses and pummeling people. When I'd get moving I was like a tractor bashing through shrubs. The nostalgia kicked in hard on the walk back. I remembered sitting in the bleachers at a pep rally, staring down at Reggie making his speech and at Joalene staring as always and then months later in the gym with her, alone, the day when Reggie went for Dora, the cheerleader with the thirty-six-inch inseam. And Dora was only five-ten. I'm six foot and my inseam's thirty-three. Dora had the wrappers on her and Joalene had the high-end pooper but the low-end legs. Legs won with

Reggie. That left me.

Most of what I think when I think about football is the afterwards part about staying in Waketon and working while Joalene went to the local college. She'd wanted to go to Notre Dame, but didn't get in, and since I didn't get a scholarship, I went to work. But the chunky kid got me thinking about football, the game, and I actually smiled to myself a few times during the walk home.

That night I slept all the way through, without even a pee break. First thing I did when I woke up was stretch. Second thing was drop down to do push-ups.

And my gut didn't touch.

I had an inch to spare—at least. So I lowered myself till my belly started to flatten against the floor, then pressed myself up. All total, at least two inches of movement. Not what most would call a push-up but more than I'd done in years. And I did six.

On the seventh rep, my arms buckled and I plopped down like a seal.

After rolling around and wiggling to my feet, and then emptying myself in the bathroom, I grabbed a slice of lasagna for breakfast. It was cold and congealed, and even though it had been in the fridge, the taste was off. So I wolfed down the last few bites and threw the other four slices into the trash. Which seemed to trigger a sudden urge to get out into the sunny day. But no walking—I'd gotten my exercise in. I was driving.

Right out of the driveway, the Corvair misfired. Black smoke spewed out of the exhaust as the car jolted. My head snapped forward, and then back as the car lurched forward. It must've shaken my brain. Maybe it was even a concussion. Because I should've headed for the river, or out through the fields to some place with open space and big skies. That's what a reasonable person would do on a sunny day. But my brain was so fritzed that I headed straight into town, towards the unnatural lair of the weirdos, where jitters attack football players and brains get double-scrambled.

13

LIBRARY SCIENCE

Susy Liu Anne says 95 percent of thought is subconscious and that I had a hankering to read whether I knew it or not. I still blame the misfire, but whatever it was that made me drive to the hill below the library was fighting hard with the more reasonable hankering for the lounger and an ice cold quart. It was a good ten minutes I sat in the Corvair staring up at the dark building with narrow windows, feeling my throat go dry, before I finally got out and shuffled up the path. At the top, I took another three minutes catching my breath, before I actually walked in.

The library was like all libraries pretty much. I guessed. I hadn't been in since the remodel just after high school. Stacks of books were off to the right and computers off to the left and more stacks of books along the back wall. A few people shuffled through the aisles, browsing. But no one spoke. The place was too quiet. Like home was without Joalene. Full of ghosts. I almost ran.

But a circular desk was in front with an information sign. A guy sat behind it, reading. So I walked up and just so I could hear a voice, I said, "Excuse me."

The guy looked up and in that shushed library voice asked me if I needed anything.

"Guys work here?" I said, softer this time. "I thought girls only for this kind of thing." He was a regular looking guy too, not some dweeb from the science team.

"I don't even wear glasses," he said.

"Hah."

"So what are you looking for?"

"I don't know. What kind of books you got?"

"All kinds. And what we don't have we can usually order."

I looked around at a woman behind a computer and at another guy reading at a desk and then up at the ceiling made of those off-white, acoustic tiles. The air vent rattled, puffing recycled air through the room, and a clock hung on the wall, digital, with red numbers all square and bold. So I asked the guy,

"You got books on Time?"

"Like *A Brief History of Time*?"

"No," I told him. "Like a real history book, not some fluff astronomy thing. Or maybe some comics. You got comics?"

"We have both."

The library guy pointed me to the physics section where

the Time books were and then to the comics section where the superheroes were. I picked up an X-Men and realized how easy they were now that I could read better. After a quick scan and noticing, just by chance, that they were still giving the female mutants big breasts and tiny waists, I headed to the calendar section and picked up a calendar book, something on the history of the calendar, and sat in the back corner in the softest chair they had, which was rock compared to the lounger. I opened the book in the middle, right at this section about a Mayan calendar, which I'd figured was the same as ours. But it's not. There's a bunch of different calendars, from all sorts of countries. The Mayan one's all about big cycles and little cycles. The big cycle ended in 2012, according to the book, which was supposed to be a big deal since it lasted five thousand years. But nothing happened. I skimmed through another section on astronomy and another on the Chinese and a few other pages here and there before an hour'd passed and I realized I'd missed my quart. So I headed back to the desk to check out a couple other calendar books I'd found.

Instead of the guy at the desk, there was a frumpy, frowning woman. And in front of her was a new sign. It read, "Now Hiring."

I asked, "The guy quit?"

"He's temp."

"So, what are you hiring for?"

"Assistant librarian and customer service."

"Two jobs?"

"One. We're a small library."

"What's he have to do?"

"Well," she said, her voice as grouchy as her face, "the *person* who is hired will have to answer questions, stack books and keep the place clean."

"Needs a degree?"

"Technically, no."

"I really want the job."

Like Susy Liu Anne says, 95 percent is subconscious—we just usually have a filter that keeps us from saying senseless things. Clearly, my filter'd been gashed. But the thing is, sometimes after you say something crazy, like "I really want the job," you start to think about it like it's a real thought. Even if it's senseless.

So the lady said, "Oh," and gave me the vertical scan with a sour face.

I looked down at my clothes and realized I was wearing my elastic pants with stained thighs and frayed knees, and that even though my gut wasn't drooping anymore like a bag of pudding, my T-shirt was stretched and faded. From looking around at the library goers, none of that should've mattered. But my greasy hair I'm sure did, and my sweaty armpits I'm sure did, and a little waft of my unshowered scent I'm sure did too. So I said, "I'll come back," and rushed out.

And I meant it, crazy as that sounds. I drove home and showered and shaved, got into the closet and pulled out my nice pants and the iron and the ironing board. I needed a shirt with a collar, too, so I reached down the rack and at the very back saw three ironed shirts that Joalene had left me, just in case I ever got off my ass.

The shirts made me not want to go back to the library. Because it was doing exactly what she wanted me to, same as I'd done practically all my life up until the last couple of years. It's not right to feel spiteful that way, I know. But it was just another one of those "you ain't nothing" slaps. I actually stared at the shirts for a few seconds, getting myself worked up, before I snatched out a blue one and cursed Joalene and put it on. I grabbed my tie, a red one, wrapped it around my neck, stood myself in front of the mirror and tied a knot. A crappy one. Too short. I tried again. Crooked. Fifteen times I tried, and I could never get any damn knot that didn't look like an ape had tied it.

I called Herm.

"You're looking for a job?"

"And I can't tie my stupid tie."

"We'll be right there."

"We?"

"You think I can tie a tie?"

So I pulled my tan pants up and buttoned the buttons and zipped up. And the pants slid right down to my butt. Good thing I had a butt or they'd have been on the floor. I pulled them up again and folded the waistband in to see how much thinner I was—three inches, easy. It was cool. Caught myself grinning. Except I didn't have more pants, not any smaller. I'd pulled the smallest pair from the plumber days. So I put a belt on and pulled it tight, and the waistband creased in three places and the belt went past the last hole. I cursed and wanted a quart, which I realized I'd forgotten again, and was heading in for number two on the day when up drove Herm and right behind him Susy Liu Anne. They both came rushing up and both waved through the window and both pounded on the door and yelled and made a full-on, head-splitting racket.

"My pants don't fit, either," I said as I opened the door while holding them up by the waistband.

Herm said, "Susy Liu Anne, you can take care of that for him too, right, honey?"

She rushed around and sped up her voice. "Did she take her sewing machine?"

"It's in the closet," I said, because I'd seen it on the ground by the shirts.

"Okay." And rapid fire: "What kind of job did you get? Where? When's your interview?"

"I don't have an interview."

Herm asked, "So why are you getting dressed up?"

"I can't walk in wearing an elastic waist. I wouldn't hire me. I got to be presentable at least."

"He's right, Herm." And to me, "Now turn around, sweetie." Susy Liu Anne started pulling at my pants and poking in pins. Then she turned me around and looked at my waist from the front. "Okay, give them to me." She held out her hand. I hesitated. "You wear boxers, don't you?" I nodded. "Then drop your trousers. I need to get back to the office."

I obeyed and handed them over.

Herm got himself a quart and me a quart and we opened them. He sat in Joalene's old chair while I sat across from him in the lounger and pulled a towel across my waist. "Sel," he asked me, as the *thrip-thrip-thrip* of the sewing machine started. "Where's the job?"

"The library," I said.

He called to Susy Liu Anne in the bedroom. "You hear that—*the library*." And to me quietly: "No shit?"

"No shit."

"Whoa."

The machine stopped. Susy Liu Anne hurried out. "The library. That's not a new bar, is it?"

"It's the one with books."

She gave Herm a long, suspicious look, and he shook his head and shrugged like he couldn't believe it either. So she said all big and overly proud, "That's wonderful, Sel," and swirled around and hurried back to the *thrip-thrip-thrip*ping.

Herm examined the lounger, the beer table beside it and the physics books I'd brought back from the library. "You really are reading this stuff, aren't you?"

"Did you know the Mayans, the Mexican people who built the pyramids in the mountains, they believe we're in this five-thousand-year cycle and that it's going to end in like two years?"

"No."

"Then everything's going to change."

"You don't believe that stuff, do you?"

"I don't know. Doesn't matter. What I'm saying is, yeah, I've been reading it, and what they say is that everyone since the beginning counted. Some counted the moons, like I said, and some counted the suns—you know, to figure a day—and some, but not many, looked up at the sky and figured, well, the moon's big and low—I guess winter's coming. And crap like that. They just looked at things that happened, and then someone started counting them."

"So they're counting. What's the big deal?"

"Because these modern guys, they got it all wrong. I don't know why, but it bothers me—that Hawking guy blabbing on about Time changing, which is kind of looney, really. Shit, Herm, this other book says that we got ourselves a different day on Earth than they do on Mars, or Venus, or any of the other planets, because they count the sun, and the other planets don't spin the same as we do. So Time's different there. And it's supposed to be something all profound." I yelled into the bedroom. "Susy Liu Anne, that book you gave me makes no sense. I think it's wrong."

She popped back out. "Of course it's wrong, Sel. Every scientist ever has been wrong. Someone else always comes along and finds something new." Then she popped back into the bedroom. "Almost there," she yelled, as she kicked on Joalene's old machine.

And I thought, *Every scientist ever. Every one's been wrong. All of them.* I yelled, "Every one?"

She yelled back, "Except for those that haven't been proved wrong yet."

I thought, *All right, so Hawking really is a loon.*

And Herm asked, as if he'd been thinking about it awhile, "You sure you want to work at the library?"

Of course I wasn't sure, now that he was asking. And before I got an answer together, he went on.

"You meet Ms. Cawstrick yet?"

"Mrs. Happy with the little mouth?"

Without even chuckling, Herm said, "The library's not necessarily the safest place to work."

"It's a library, Herm."

And he got quiet, and fiddly with the arm of his chair. "You're right."

"Dogs aren't allowed, are they?" One scratch of cur dog's back didn't mean I wouldn't splat another yippie thing with a stack of encyclopedias.

"No dogs."

"Good."

Herm took a swig. "I was just talkin'."

And like it used to after a big game, my stomach got to rumbling. I asked Herm, "Should we get a pizza?"

"Nah. Won't be a few minutes. She works fast."

"You're right," I said. "I shouldn't eat anyway." And swigged my beer instead.

Next thing I knew, Susy Liu Anne was out and holding my pants and snatching my beer. "You can't drink that before an interview."

I said, "Wha…?" But before I could get it all out, she'd shoved the pants at me, slid into the kitchen and dumped my practically full quart into the sink. "Hey, what are you doing?"

She snapped at me: "Try them on."

I did. The pants fit better than I remembered, even new.

"She's a magician, Herm."

"Stop that," she said, and shoved the tied tie at me that I slipped over my head. Once Susy Liu Anne had pulled the tie tight and adjusted my shirt and pants, she walked over beside Herm and together they gave me the scan.

"You look all right," said Herm.

"Very handsome," said Susy Liu Anne. "I just know you'll get that job."

"That makes one of us."

"Two," said Herm.

"Great. You're a team."

Susy Liu Anne glided to my side, took my arm in a dainty vice grip and with a soft, "I know you won't let us down, Sel," shoved me out the door.

14

A WOMAN WITH PULL

I got to the library, gave my pits a pat down with an old T-shirt, and headed up the hill. At the top again, I took a few minutes to recover, then a couple big breaths to ease my nerves, and walked in. The temp guy was back and the job sign still there, so I walked up and told him, "I'm here to apply for the job."

"You finished with Time?" he said.

"No," I said. "Just finished with the days on the lounger."

"Ah." He pulled an application from the drawer, handed it to me and told me to fill it out and bring it back.

While I was filling it out at an open table, Ms. Cawstrick walked up and sat down and whispered, "Excuse me."

I said, "Hello," and smiled even though she'd been sour

before.

She asked, "Is your name Sel Ray Bob?"—separating the syllables.

"All one word," I said. "Yes, ma'am."

"You're friends with Ms. Poderosa?"

"Who?"

"Susy Liu Anne Poderosa."

"Oh, yeah. She still uses that."

"And you are friends?"

"She fixed my pants," I said. "And tied my tie." I tugged on it for emphasis.

"Come with me."

Ms. Cawstrick stood, and I stood, and she told me to bring the application, which I'd already forgotten. I followed her between two stacks, through a door in the back and into a small office. She closed the door and walked around a little wooden desk and sat on an old wooden chair. "Sit," she said.

I sat on another wooden chair across from her.

"Here." She held out her open hand. "Pass that to me."

So I gave her the half-complete application, and she scanned it and then told me, "Okay."

I said, "What's okay?"

"We're going to hire you."

"You're going to hire me?"

"Yes."

"Wow. Cool." Because it was. No procedures or anything. No interview. No nothing but the application. So I said, "Why?"

"You come highly recommended."

"By Susy Liu Anne?"

"Yes."

"Too bad she wasn't my crush."

"Excuse me?"

I shut myself up. Because I'd just blurted. Again. First it was, "I really want the job," and then the crush blurt. Two blurts—something I hadn't done since, basically forever. I wasn't a blurter. I wasn't a talker much for that matter, but to blurt out my thoughts, my underneath ones about wants and feelings and crap—that got me a bit unsettled and I got a hankering for a quart. Until I got to wondering how it was that Susy Liu Anne had so much pull. So I answered Ms. Cawstrick, "Nothing." And then, "Does Susy Liu Anne work for the city?"

"Not directly. But she's an acquaintance, and I trust her completely." She dipped her head so she was looking up at me, and full of suspicion said, "You will not betray that trust, will you, Mr. Selraybob?"

"No, ma'am. No. I won't. Not at all."

Three days later, I started the job.

First thing I did, after the temp, Alvin, showed me the desk and drawers and how to fill out forms for new library cards and what all the numbers on all the books meant and how to figure them out, was to check out the Time section and leaf through a couple of Time books. But I didn't get much chance to read the first couple weeks because I was constantly finding books for people and putting them away and dusting counters and answering questions about the Internet, which I'd used at Herm's a few times, but had to learn how to set up. I had to learn and relearn everything Alvin told me. Basically, I was working. And that's not why I was there, I realized. I was there for the books and reading. I would've quit after the third week if it hadn't been for the chunky kid from the football field.

He walked in all sullen and head down with his none-too-happy and extra-stout mother. The first thing the kid did when he saw me, after his eyes went big and wide, was drop a couple of steps behind his mother and drop down into a squat with his arms out. I almost yelped in excitement. He only did one, real fast, because his mom caught him and whipped around scowling and grabbed his shirt. But I couldn't stop smiling. The thing is, the kid was smiling too, even though he was being yanked half off his feet. So we caught eyes smiling and, I don't know…it was a good moment.

I watched them for a while wandering up and down the aisle, looking for something, but confused of course, by the numbers. So I got up and walked over to the kid and asked them if there was anything I could help them with.

The woman said, "He wants a football book." And by her sour voice, she was none too pleased about it.

I thought it was pretty cool. "He does?" I said.

"Yes," said the kid. "By a lineman." Then louder and higher pitched. "A tackle."

"Ah. Yes. The most important position."

"I don't know where he got this football idea from. He

just wants to go to the park." And to the kid: "You used to be such a good student."

"You got to study," I told him.

"Football players don't study."

"I do now."

"Why?" he asked.

"Because," I told him, "I got something stuck in my craw."

"Like a chicken wing."

"Nope. Not even a stalk of broccoli."

"I hate broccoli."

"Me too."

"Uch." His face was all scrinched up and his tongue out.

Fast as I could I said, "I'm talking about an idea, you know, a thought. One day I was driving by and saw the library sign and all the sudden realized that this thought in my craw was in the books, or at least there were a lot of books about the thought I had stuck in my craw."

As if he'd figured me out, the kid said, "You were thinking about football."

"Physics," I said. "Well not really physics, but like it. But you want a football book, right?"

"If I gotta read, yeah."

"You have to read," said his mother.

"Over here then." So I went back to my sour boss and asked her where the football books were, then led the mom and son to the proper aisle and looked through a few books. But they were all by running backs and quarterbacks and prima donna's who'd sexed around and talked cocky.

"Tell you what," I said. "I can order books. So I'll look through the catalog and see what we got. I'll find one."

"By a tackle."

"Carl...It's Carl, right?"

"Yeah."

"The thing is, Carl, what the left tackles in the world need, really badly, is someone who doesn't just play football, but who can write and tell everyone how cool it is to be a left tackle. Because, believe it or not, sometimes you get the girl." And I gave him the big nod that felt like a lie. Because they were leftover girls. I sure didn't want to tell him leftover girls, so with the mom glaring me down, I went on. "But writers are the ones who get even more girls than quarterbacks."

"No they don't."

"Oh yeah. Lots more. But I tell you, a left tackle writer would be a double bonus." The mother eased eased up with my writer talk, but I can't say the kid was all excited. So I told him, "You can start with the reading and go from there. I'll look for a book."

The kid said, "Thanks."

And the mom said, "Thank you." And when she did it was different. I felt forgiveness. As if I'd been guilty of talking football, on top of quitting football, getting fat, being unsuccessful, ruining Joalene's life, and killing little Lexie because I was watching the traffic instead of the blind man. It was awful.

I found one book by a left tackle, but it was a short

book and about religion mostly, which I wasn't so sure was what he wanted. And there was another one, not by a left tackle, but about linemen-type things. I did find one, by a reporter guy, that had a whole big section about a left tackle, who'd been homeless, and who was big and fat and finally went pro. I didn't read it, but I figured that would be the best. I got them all, just in case.

It was a good thing, too. The first thing the kid did when he came back was walk right up and ask if I had a book for him. So I pulled the three out and told him they were the only ones I found. "You can write one," I told him.

He said, "Thanks," and took the books and looked at them and just stood in front of the desk awhile, not moving and not reading either.

So I said, "Hey. I got a break in fifteen minutes."

"You do?"

"I do. You bring your homework?"

"Yeah," he said.

"Well, do your homework, then we can go out to the hill out front and I can show you some moves if you want."

"Yeah?"

"But only if you want. If you don't, then no problem. I got my calendar book to read."

"No," he said. "That'd be cool."

"Good."

"I been doing the squats." The kid actually puffed up his chest.

"I see."

"Every day. Or almost."

"That's all right. It's good. Are you feeling them?"

He squeezed his thigh. "I guess," he said. But he didn't look so sure. "Maybe a little."

"Give it time," I said. "You got a year to go before next season."

"Six months, more like. They start in summer."

"More than enough," I said, and pointed to a table. "But fifteen minutes to break."

I did some rearranging of books and answered the phone a couple of times, and after fifteen minutes Carl and I headed out and along the path to the hill. Instead of walking down the sidewalk, I headed down the side, practically dragging Carl with me, and right away at the bottom turned and walked up. It was a short hill, not a mountain but a good hill, where the sledders come after a snow. At a good pace it's about a minute walk up, but at our pace—or my pace—it was a three-minute huff and puff. Carl was huffing and puffing by the top with me. We both bent over with our hands on our knees and he said, "You don't exercise, do you?"

I shook my head.

"You're slower than I am."

I nodded. "Again," I said, heaving a breath, and turned and headed down the hill. He watched and I said, "Come on. If I can, you can."

He came and we walked down the hill and back up and huffed and puffed. My break was up though, so we headed back in, and I told him, "Tomorrow, same time if you want."

"I don't know." Carl was still huffing for air.

"Here," I said, and quickly I showed him the squat and twist move by getting low and shoving out with the hands. "For when they're off balance. You get 'em off balance and you can shove 'em anywhere. But you got to keep your shoulders down. That's very important. You can't be scrunching up your neck. That's when you get weak."

"No scrunching," he said while he imitated me.

"Good," I told him. "So, tomorrow."

"We walking the hill?"

"We're doing some reading in the library, and yeah, we're walking the hill."

"And more moves."

"Strength first."

"I don't know." He looked away and down and over at his books. "I might have stuff to do after school."

"Well," I said. And I rubbed my gut and smiled down at Carl. "I'm walking the hill. You can come if you want."

He did. For the next couple of weeks I sat and read calendar books, maybe ten pages a day in between library duties and Ms. Cawstrick's glares, and Carl and I did the hill and a few squats and a couple of push-ups in the dirt. It wasn't much of a workout, but fifteen minutes a day isn't so bad. It's a start. And I'd taken to doing morning push-ups as well. And I'd bought some raw spinach and made a salad one night at home. It was sickening grass, and I needed a pizza and a quart to wash it down. But it was a start, too.

I found myself moving faster around the library. Getting the books put up and the shelves rearranged before I was even supposed to start work. Crazy son of a bitch I'd become, showing up early. And I read more and faster, I swear. And my pants were loose again. So I called Herm.

Herm asked me how work was going. I told him, "All right, just like yesterday. Except I've been showing up early." He told me what a crazy son of a bitch I'd become and that Susy Liu Anne was getting on him to be more productive with his life now that I had a job and all.

That afternoon he stopped by the library a few minutes before break. It was snowing, the first one of December, and Carl was at his desk and I was behind mine when Herm walked up and asked me if I'd been drinking my quarts. I told him, "After work. Yes sir. One a day."

"Nub-brained son of a bitch," he said. "You need three."

I hushed him, and Carl walked up and said, "It's snowing."

I said, "I got my boots."

"It's cold."

"Rain, sleet, snow. That's why football players are tougher than the baseball boys who quit once it gets slippery. We're going." I stood.

Herm looked down at Carl. "So this is the tackle?"

"It is," I said. And I gave Herm the vertical scan, and to Carl I said, "You think his skinny legs can make it up the hill with us?"

So Carl gave Herm the vertical scan. "I don't know," he said, shaking his head. "It's steep."

"I don't know either," I said. "Let's go." So Carl and I headed out into the snow while Herm watched. "You coming?" I asked. Herm shrugged and joined and we walked the hill in the snow, the three guys. Carl led. And I noticed that while Herm and I were panting a bit, Carl wasn't. Not after the first climb. So when we got back down for number two, I told him, "Okay. Run the last bit. Just to see how it goes."

"Okay," he said. "'Cause it's easy walking now. Even with the slipping." He grinned. To Herm he said, "It wasn't so easy at first. But now it is." And he pulled up his shirt and showed his belt cinched in and his pants' waist creased in like a pleat. I did the same, and Carl and I stood side by side with the white flakes falling and our shirts up, grinning all proud at Herm, who'd never had to worry once about downsizing his gut.

15

The History of Time
According to Selraybob

As my gut thinned and the reading got faster, my head puffed up full of Time information about calendars and counting and how right I was and how wrong that Hawking guy was. He was making something simple totally complex. It's like the library sometimes—we got all this stuff around us telling us how to make more money and drive faster and eat right and live right and go to church right, when there isn't much better in the world than hanging out on the couch with your sweetie and holding her hand. Which, of course, I wasn't doing at all because she'd skipped out with Sir Hairless Calves. But I guess I've got a sappy streak. I'll keep it down. It shouldn't be hard. What I'm saying though is, if we just thought simple and sappy, we'd see how basic Time is. But we start thinking too much. And reading too much. But that's what happens when you get something stuck in your craw—it doesn't dissolve and slide down to your stomach. It sticks back there behind your molars and you got to dig around for a long while to get it out. And hopefully, if you're lucky, your thoughts don't all get regurgitated on your buddy. Like what happened to me when I went by Herm's later that week. He wanted to shoot me.

The sun was out and the air dry and warm and it felt like spring in January. Global warming, according to the news, but spring days, no matter the date, meant Susy Liu Anne's wicker rockers and sitting and sipping a quart or two on Herm's front porch. We started out talking about the oak in his front yard and the squirrels, then we switched to saying nothing, which is as good as talking when you're sitting outside with a buddy and a beer. Then mid-quart, because my craw was busting over with thoughts, I started in about how the first calendars had to do with the seasons—the season to harvest, the season to plant, cold season and hot season. "They weren't written down back then. You had to look up at the stars and sun and planets to know when it was. Then some people decided they wanted to know more. So they started tracking the sun and the solstices, which is when the days are the longest and shortest, and the equinoxes, which are when the daylight equals the night light."

"I know those, Sel."

"I didn't. Or I'd forgotten. But what the ancient guys did was figure out that there were two of each and then used those to measure change. So those days were big deals, and really the only days with names for a while. That's why, I figure, so many big events in history seemed to happen on the solstice. Like Christ's birth."

"Don't be goin' into Christ's birth."

"I'm not going into anything."

"Sounds like you are."

"I'm talking Time, Herm. And history."

"I already feel guilty enough just askin' my start-of-the-world question."

"And I'm just telling you what's in the books. That's all. Same as them at the church. They're just telling you what's in the Good Book."

"Don't be goin' into the Good Book neither."

I was shocked. He'd snapped that out so fast, giving me the scowl of death with it, that I stopped the rocker and started blurting. "All I'm saying is that there's this science guy, from one of my calendar books—I don't remember which—but he says that originally everyone said Christ was born on the spring equinox. But that's too much a sex time, with all the mating rituals going on and pairing up and heading out behind the rock for some of the sweaty and slick."

"Damn, Sel. Christ was born on Christmas." Then he took a swig of his beer while I kept blurting.

"Right. Because Christ's a Northern Hemisphere guy, and winter's cold, so they had to get him away from the sexing time. So they moved his birthday to the winter solstice, which used to be on the twenty-fifth back then, because all these numbers they put to days are all made up anyway."

"It'd be better if you just drank your quart."

"Yeah." I took a swig but couldn't shut up. "I'm just telling you what the science guy said."

"No, Sel." Herm stood up and gave me the downward glare. "You're tellin' me what you think. And usin' the science guy as an excuse. Because if you agree with what someone else says, then it's yours." And with that he got up. "You want chips or somethin'?"

"I'm good. Thanks."

"All right."

"Sorry."

Herm went in and I sat outside on the rocker thinking about thinking, which was double tiring. So I cut out half and started looking at the sun heading down, and I got to remembering the day people. The sun comes up—that's a day. They're the day people. What you'd figure is that someone would have counted the days from solstice to solstice and figured, okay, we got 365—let's call that a year. Which they kind of did. But people, I'm learning, always have to break things up into pieces, like split up just because he's not perfect, so you leave the imperfect half on the lounger and go off chasing someone perfect. At least to her. Some dream-quarterback business puke with shaved friggin' calves and a waxed chest.

Luckily, Herm walked back out with his bowl of potato chips and a glass of bourbon. And I tried like hell to force myself away from Joalene and back to Time. So I asked

Herm, "How come the day people and the year people never seemed to have met?"

"Hell, Sel, why you even askin' me?"

"I'm just saying—you got the people who look at the solstices and seasons and count that way, and you got the day watchers who count another way. And they never seemed to have gotten together on things. It doesn't make sense."

"You ever goin' to be quiet?"

"It's either Time or Joalene. Which do you want?" Because Joalene was way too close to the surface, and my quart was warming up and my stomach was churning. I had to spill something.

And Herm knew. He gave me that closed-eye and fed-up head shake and told me, "Just leave out the Good Book."

"All right," I said, and blabbed on about calendars. "So some year-person decided to break it up into months. Gregory did that. That's why we call the calendar we use now the Gregorian calendar. At first there were ten months, and they had thirty days. I mean, geeminy—a nimwit would've figured out that everything was going to get off from the equinoxes and solstices. After a while the months got so far off that December, which comes from the Latin word for *ten*, was in the middle of summer. So finally another emperor came along—Augustus—and he decided that December was a cold month, dammit. So it's got to be moved. 'Move it back,' he said. So he added a bunch of days into the middle of the year, and everyone had to hang out and count these filler days that weren't on a regular calendar and would never come again. They just pushed the months back. But Augustus was smarter than Gregory. He knew you needed more months to keep it working, so he added two, August and July, named for himself and Julius—they were very modest men. That seemed to be the emperor way—modesty. Humble and modest. And jealous. The emperors that came after got a little pissed off at Julius and Augustus and started renaming months after themselves, which screwed things all up. They never knew when they were. One day it's September the fifth, and the next day it's Marcusmonth the sixth. Luckily that didn't work out and some emperor without a volcano-sized ego came in and set the calendar back the way it was with only July and August and the original ten. But still things got off, like they always do. So after a while they had to come up with extra days every four years and make leap years."

I paused, and Herm nodded, thinking I was done. I wasn't.

"And then, on the other side of the world you got the Chinese."

"Aw, Jesus, Sel."

"Just listen," I said. "They didn't much go for the sun thing. They counted the moons instead. The way I see it, the Chinese were kind of like the Greeks, even though they don't look much alike. They both realized that we're the ones moving around the sun. See, the Chinese chose the moon because it was the moving piece. That's why you hear about all those parades during December or some other month but not on New Year's. And with a different animal all the time. Which is probably the coolest thing they did—label all the years with animals. It makes for an awesome parade."

Herm said, "Let's talk diapers."

"Diapers?"

"Yeah, diapers. You wanna talk—we'll talk diapers."

"You're selling diapers now?"

"Cotton ones, with a lining."

"Really?"

"They're fantastic, Sel. The best damn diapers ever."

"But diapers, Herm. Why not socket wrenches?"

"A thing's a thing. Don't matter what it is so long as it can be sold."

"I guess you're right."

"I am," he said.

"I am too. I swear. All this calendar crap, it's all just a bunch of counting and dividing and naming. That's all Time's ever been. That's all I'm saying. It's the philosophizing people who go and try to add meaning to our changes. So they put Time in, and then the past and the future and the Now become some mystical sacred things that you can't argue about or you're called crazy. That's all I'm saying. And now I'll shut up."

"Shit, Sel. You never talked so much in your life."

"Just had to empty my craw."

"Is it empty? I sure hope it's empty."

"Not even a niblet," I said.

"Finally. Now you want another quart?"

"That'd be good." Because I was already missing my full craw.

16

CONSPIRACY IN THE CRAW

It wasn't that my knees ached from being crammed underneath the desk or that the schoolkids liked to rearrange the comics every afternoon. It wasn't that I put them back wrong, twice, and got reprimanded for it three times. And it wasn't that half my high school football team and their girlfriends and wives and tykes walked in after church one day and smiled down at me behind the desk and all cheery said, "Hey...Sel?"

"Yeah," I said.

Then, all dragged out with shock and mockery, they chimed in with, "Surprised to see ya here at the books," and a team laugh.

And it wasn't that Zach, the backup running back who'd gotten himself a Volvo sports sedan and a good job and a long-haired wife with thin hips, felt like adding, "Just joking, Sel. It's good to see you. Tell Joalene hello. Y'all are still together, aren't you?"

Joy.

But none of that's what was getting to me. I'm not saying the library was heaven, but Carl was a good kid, the customers were friendly, and even Ms. Cawstrick's reprimands were overly polite.

It was my craw. Ever since Herm's porch, my craw'd started to go slick and slimy. Thoughts that used to stick, like during my epiphanic flood, didn't stick anymore. The only thoughts big enough to wedge themselves in were about Joalene, like about the house being quiet and how good the lasagna had been and how I wished I hadn't thrown it out after the second slice, since it was a nice thing for her to do really.

I needed something new. Something that would stick again. Something cool that wasn't Joalene and the lounger and had nothing to do with high school or Waketon even.

I tried, too. I read about dust, which is mostly skin if you're inside a lot, which meant that skin was passing down my gullet all day—and the last thing I wanted was to ruminate on a dusty gullet. Another day I read about furniture making and another day about cooking—those things just brought back up lost jobs, dead dogs and Joalene. I tried memorizing the Dewey library code, and did all right for a couple of days, but like with all memorizing, once you learn it, you're done. Last thing I did was ask Ms. Cawstrick what was in her craw, like what kept her going from day to day.

"My yard," she told me. "I like to mow."

Loon. Mowing's the worst thing about summer.

What happened finally was that a week after the joyous high school reunion, I was sitting behind the desk with a calendar book open, hoping an ancient calendar war or sex scandal or something else new and amazing would pop its way into my craw, when in walked that skinny punk Time-fixer wannabe who'd been watching the shop for Joalene's favorite Sphere of Time. This punk shop watcher saw me skimming the book and walked up and grinned and said, "Hey. Still looking up Time stuff?"

I said, "Yeah," all quick and tough and a little pissed off, like a mafia guy. "I'm still looking things up. You still subbing for the ones who fix clocks?"

He leaned over the desk, glanced down at my book. "Calendars, man. You'll find nothing there."

"What's it matter?" I said.

"I'm just saying, if you want to know Time, like catch a clue about what the big deal is, you got to see the source."

"There's no source of Time."

"There's a source, all right." He glanced around as if looking for cops and lowered his voice. "The center of the conspiracy."

Flip job that the guy was, the only thing that'd been having any traction in my craw was Joalene, as if she had Velcro-covered arms and spikes sticking out her back. So I kept him going. "The conspiracy," I said. "Right."

"It's real."

"So which center are you talking about?"

The guy bent low and scanned the room and without even looking at me started whispering. "Colorado, man. Boulder. Right in the center of the country. That's where they keep the atomic clock, the true source, so they can beam it out in all directions."

"The atomic clock?" I asked.

He jutted his chin at my book. "You've read about it, I'm sure."

"Of course," I said. "Yeah."

And I had read about it. Somewhere. But it was all blabber about cesium atoms and resonant frequencies. So I'd kind of skimmed.

Right then, though, while I was trying to picture the atomic clock and remember how it ticked, in walked the two dark and brooding clock fixers, side by side, same height, same big noses, same black eyes. They passed together and nodded at the watcher, and the watcher put on a feeble smile and nodded back.

"I met them," I told the watcher.

"Where?" he asked, all the sudden suspicious as hell.

"At their shops."

"Oh yeah. Right." He went all fidgety but didn't look back. "They go back into the books?"

They'd stopped in the near stacks, in the romance section, and with their heads cocked down but eyes staring straight at us, not even trying to hide their glares.

"Nope," I said. "They're watching you."

"They're following me."

"Why?"

"Why do you think? They're the muscle of the Time fixers."

I still didn't get it. He went on.

"Hamayans, man. The worst."

"Hamayans?"

"You really don't know, do you? Shit. You're so ignorant. Hamayan—half Hawaiian, half Mayan."

"Like the hula Hawaiians?"

He leaned in, squeezing in a yell so hard that his eyes went buggy and bloodshot. "No, man. Like the end-of-the-world Mayans."

"Oh, yeah." I shut my book. "But nothing happened."

"Not yet." He glanced behind him. One of the Hamayans smiled, and it wasn't any "How about a beer?" kind of happy smile. A bit evil, really. More like they were selling poison taffy at the carnival. So the watcher went whisper-blurting. "Look. All I'm saying is that the Colorado people know the whole story. It's at the atomic clock. Go to the source, man. Go to the source." Then he glanced back again to where the Hamayans had been, but weren't anymore. "Crap," he said. And to me: "You want to know, you gotta go. Colorado, man. Boulder, Colorado." With that, he ducked around and rushed out.

I sat there trying to figure out where the Hamayans had gone. I wasn't sure if they'd slipped out before the watcher or ducked behind the computers, except I checked there, and they hadn't. I walked the stacks and kids books too, and even looked behind the checkout counter, but not a sign. All I knew was that they were gone and that my craw was filling up with something not exactly Time but a hell of a lot better than mulling over eleven years of substitution.

What's more, that afternoon I was driving past the Mexican joint. The Corvair was rumbling pretty good, and I looked over, half expecting to see the Hamayans, but instead saw Joalene walk out with the same gelled-hair business puke. She looked around all slinky and showy and spied me, and for a second I swear I saw her checking out my collared shirt. It was quick though, and lickety-split she looked away and said something to the guy, probably something about hiding from her stalking ex or some excuse like that, and rushed back inside. The gelled-hair guy—and probably waxed-back too—gave me and the Corvair a good once-over as I slowed down and let the engine rumble nice and easy before heading on down the street to Herm's.

"Pack up," I told him.

"I ain't goin' nowhere."

"Yeah you are."

Susy Liu Anne walked in from the laundry and asked me where I was going.

"To see the clock," I said.

"Which clock?"

"The atomic one. It's in Boulder."

"I didn't hear about this. Herm, honey, why haven't I heard about this?"

Herm told her, "Don't matter. I'm not goin'."

Asian Southern women can look ferocious, and she gave him the glare of the dragon witch. "I," she told him, "want to go to Boulder."

As if retarded, Herm asked her, "You wanna drive cross-country?"

"You heard me. Yes." And to me, sweetly: "How far is it, Sel?"

"It's a ways."

Herm was quick. "Twelve hours at least. Fourteen more like—we gotta cross Missouri *and* Kansas."

"Can we make it in a weekend? Are they open on weekends? Probably not. We'll need to have a tour." She was getting herself excited. "How about we leave Sunday, early-early? We'll move the weekend. Herm can work anywhere. As long as you have your computer, right, honey?" Herm scowled. Susy Liu Anne rolled on. "I can take off Monday and Tuesday, and maybe Wednesday. A road trip. This is going to be great."

Herm glared while Susy Liu Anne took a deep breath to slow herself down. She ended her spiel with, "Sel, let them know you're taking a few days off."

"They're not going to let me off."

"Of course they will, sweetheart." As if she knew the answer I'd get. Which she did know, of course—yes. "I'll make chicken."

Herm's eyes went big and his mouth sagged in a pout. "You're gonna cook your once-a-year chicken?"

"This is a worthy occasion, I do believe."

"What about my birthday?"

"Have I ever not taken care of you on your birthday?"

Herm couldn't challenge that one. "No," he said. "You

always took good care of me."

Susy Liu Anne walked over and patted his cheek. "I'll cook it twice this year, and a little something extra on your special day."

"Better be extra special."

"Don't you worry."

Herm smiled. "But I'm takin' my phone."

"Of course, honey. For emergencies."

She kissed him. Then he turned to me, suddenly cheery. "You hear that—the once a year roasted feast?"

"I like roasted," I told her.

Which got Herm agitated. "This ain't just roasted, Sel! A touch of the sweet. Some spices injected in—with a needle. It's the best damn chicken in the country. You won't be able to eat that mart stuff no more. I tell you."

"Okay then," I said. "The Susy Liu Anne twice-a-year special."

She was all grins. "We'll take the Lincoln."

"Perfect," I said. Because while the Corvair has a back seat, you don't pack three people, particularly if one is me, into a precious baby and take her a thousand miles in the middle of winter. You take your buddy's wife's Lincoln.

17

ROAD TRIP TO THE SOURCE OF TIME

That night I set the alarm, and Saturday morning, early, before the sun, I woke to the buzzer. As fast as a flinch I slammed it off, then lay there for a while before forcing myself out of bed and into the shower.

Herm and Susy Liu Anne showed up a few minutes later with the Town Car. I threw on clothes and put some in a bag and went outside. Herm opened the trunk and showed me the cooler. "Homemade chicken sandwiches, chicken burritos, chicken pieces to nibble on, chips and fruit and vegetables and all sorts of sodas, and I put two six-packs in the trunk, plus a case of quarts for you."

I gave him a pat on the back. He smiled at me proudly and then in at his wife, the maker of the feast, and we got in the car and headed for Boulder.

Herm drove. Bad idea for Herm to drive, which is why I never let him drive the Corvair. He liked semi-trucks. He'd go stoner behind one, as if they were some spinning spiral thing that sent him into a stupor, which is how he was behind this 18-wheeler with smiling-Satan mud flaps.

"Herm," I said, hitting his shoulder. "See that truck?"

He said, "Huh."

"The truck, Herm. Ease off."

"Oh, yeah."

That's when the rock, a mini boulder more like, bounced from under the left Satan, took a quick tumble off the street and flew up into the air like a jagged, death-bringing asteroid and, I swear, veered midair towards the windshield. Susy Liu Anne shrieked and Herm yelled, "*Oh shit!*" and ducked. As he ducked, he yanked the wheel. The car swerved. I went tumbling in the back. And the next thing I heard, with just enough time to picture myself on a hospital bed, in a coma, with a tube down my throat and my left leg missing, was the crack of glass and a bounce over the roof. The tires skidded. I kept tumbling while Herm kept cursing. Town Cars don't roll the way SUVs do, but two wheels were off the ground. One more wrong jerk or a lurch by me in the wrong direction and we were going to go side over side down the highway.

But the next instant, together, as if some sort of mind meld occurred, Susy Liu Anne snatched the wheel while Herm pressed on the brakes. The car straightened, slowed, and seconds later, which seemed like an hour, we were stopped off the shoulder with cars speeding by.

I swear, all I heard was the rumble and swoosh of the passing semis, like tornados. Even the midget cars sounded like tanks. Everything was at level eleven—my eyes too. The windshield had spider-webbed from corner to corner in this most amazing crystal-like pattern. And with the morning light just starting to shine, rainbows reflected off of Susy Liu Anne's shiny black hair. It was beautiful. Almost like being on a real psychedelic trip. Which I might have been for a second, because I was thinking, *Whoa, I'll bet this is how it was for the Beatles, talking about Lucy in the Sky—they'd had their windshield hit by a Satan-chucked boulder, but instead of shattering the glass, it spun out a massive web. And Ringo'd been in back staring and tripping and telling them in his bloody English accent how bloody amazing it was.*

Susy Liu Anne spoke first. "We can't drive with it like this."

Herm said, "Yeah, I know," half in shock.

I said, "Yeah."

Herm said, "We almost died."

"Yeah."

"It was a good try."

Susy Liu Anne whacked him across the shoulder—not the way I had, as a nudge, but as a bruise-giving set of knuckles. "We are not quitting," she told him. Then she twisted and leaned back over the seat. "Are you quitting, Sel? Because I'm not. If you want to go, we'll go. I want to see the clock."

"The window's busted," I said.

"No one's dead, right? No one's hurt?"

I grabbed my legs, making double sure they were both

there, and said, "No." Herm shook his head.

"It's still early," Susy Liu Anne said. We'll get the windshield fixed." Then directly to Herm: "Won't we, sweetheart? We'll run to that repair shop."

"I can't drive nowhere," he said. "There's three of everything."

"They'll come to us then, won't they?" She was perking up. "Isn't that what they do, Sel? Don't the windshield guys come to the car?"

Herm grumbled. "We're on the highway."

"We'll get off the highway. Stay off the road and take the next exit. They'll come. I'll call. Go, Herm."

That's what he did. We eased the car up the shoulder to the exit and pulled off into the dirt. Susy Liu Anne called the repair shop, and the windshield people told us to sit tight. We got out and sat on the curb with a field of weeds behind us. While we sat, Susy Liu Anne opened the trunk and pulled out the chicken—smart woman. Shut Herm's grumbling up. Calmed my nerves, too. We ate for the two hours while they fixed the windshield, and then we headed out with blue tape around the seams and orders to keep it dry for two days. "Lest it leak," said the unshaven window man holding the heat gun. "It leaks: you got no warranty." He shook his head. "You pay. That's the way it is. It leaks, you pay."

After cursing and paying, Herm hopped in and peeled out. Thirty minutes later, at ten-fifteen, a strand of tape came loose and began to *plap* on the roof—*plap-plap-plap-plap*. Banging and *plap*ping and Herm was cursing the goddamn smiling-Satan truck. "We don't need to go. Sel. You don't really need to go."

I didn't respond, and Susy Liu Anne was none too happy about it. "Would you rather go back, sit by the window at the Steak 'n Shake, and wait for Joalene to saunter by with another overrated quarterback trying to relive his youth?"

"He'd have shaved calves," I said.

Herm said, "Reggie never shaved his calves."

"He probably waxes."

Herm was turning belligerent. "Next exit I'm turning around."

"She moved on anyway," I said. "Found a new quarterback." I was talking about Joalene, of course.

"I'm still turning around."

Susy Liu Anne leaned over the seat and gave me the angry-side-of-the-South glare. "What's it going to be, Sel? No more doubts. All the way or nowhere. You've got to decide now, sweetheart."

So with Susy Liu Anne fuming in front and Herm grumbling and glaring at the road, I pictured that gelled-hair prick back home gloating to Joalene about how I could barely make it a hundred miles out of town before turning around and Joalene nodding and nodding how right he was. I even pictured Carl looking down at me from the top of the hill asking if my heart was about to give out not even halfway up.

I told Herm, "I need to go."

Susy Liu Anne perked up. "You hear that, honey? You

are going to Colorado."

"Great," said Herm, grumbling again. "Fantastic."

She patted his leg.

And that was that.

Flipped as it sounds, it was fortuitous, as they say, that the windshield cracked. Because, if it hadn't, and if the new windshield didn't require two days for the seals to solidify, we wouldn't have had blue tape covering the seams between the new windshield and the black metal Lincoln. The tape wouldn't have worked its way loose, like I said, in the freeway wind, flopping around the top of the car like a broken-winged finch beneath a crow's nest. We would not, at the sight of distant heavy gray clouds and descending gray mist, have stopped four times to reattach the blue tape. Herm wouldn't have driven into the rain, worried that water would flood through the windshield into their most expensive possession. He wouldn't have rolled down the window and pressed the tape down then ducked back in, wet-headed and cursing. He would not have noticed sudden heart palpitations, pulled beneath an underpass, cursed again the rain, the wind, his heart, and the trip. Susy Liu Anne would not have kissed Herm's cheek, told him how much she loved his supportive nature, and ordered him to the passenger side. And we would not have averaged eighty, including stops, the next three hours, through downpour and *plip-plap*ping tape and drenched arms, until finally we came into the sun and Susy Liu Anne said as sharply as a Mississippi girl can, "Fucking tape." Then she pulled over, stepped out, dropped her high heels, climbed on the hood, and before Herm and I could even think to move, she was standing legs spread before the windshield, yanking the tape from around the windows and flinging it over her head.

Half-stupefied, Herm said, "Isn't she amazing?"

"Amazing," I repeated, just as stupefied.

"Yeah."

"Yeah," I said.

"And I'm married to her."

"You are."

"Yeah."

We could see the muscles in her thighs and in her arms flexing with each bend and pull. And with the last strip of tape, she took one step and leaped from the hood and onto the ground, landing smooth and easy like a ninja.

"Wow," I said.

"Amazing."

"She is," I said. And she was. It was a hell of a sight.

18

WELCOME TO NIST

I woke up the next morning nine hundred miles from home, alone in a big cushy bed in a highfalutin hotel that was old and brick and famous supposedly for being old and brick. But it was a nice damn hotel, with dark wood stairs and leather chairs all over and a stained-glass ceiling that arched over the lobby—a perfect place for a getaway with your sweetheart. It's just a good thing that Herm and Susy Liu Anne didn't come waltzing in holding hands and lovey as hell. That would've made for a rough morning.

I got lucky—they called instead. So after a hot shower, I bundled up and headed downstairs to meet the couple who'd decided to treat me to my mountain luxury. "Oh, sweetheart," said Susy Liu Anne when I thanked her again for the room. "You earned it."

"I could've stayed at a Super 8."

"You buy breakfast and see that clock; that'll be payment enough." She squeezed my arm and let go with a gentle rub.

"Okay," I said.

The snow had come down pretty good while we slept and was still coming down, but lightly, so the roads were clear and the trees heavy with tiny white mountain ranges running along the branches. It was a short walk to this little yellow-house restaurant for a Cajun breakfast. I had catfish and eggs, which, with this butter sauce poured over it, was darn near the best combination for breakfast I'd ever had. That and some Cajun coffee, which wasn't so bad at all, picked me up and actually put me in the mood for some Time conspiracy investigation.

That's when Susy Liu Anne asked, "When's the tour?"

"I don't know," I said.

So she called NIST, the National Institute of Standards and Technology, which I did know was where the clock was, while Herm and I waited and watched her sweet-talk some guy on the phone. But when her face turned from Southern belle to a frown and she put her hand over the phone and gave me the get-off-the-lounger glare, I knew I'd screwed up. "Sel," she said, extra slow. "Did you make an appointment?"

"There's no tour?" I asked her.

"No, Sel. You need to have an appointment."

"Oh."

"And we don't have one."

"Because I didn't make one."

That's when Herm started chirping. "How the hell didn't you know there weren't tours?"

"I didn't check. Okay?"

"No shit you didn't check."

Susy Liu Anne hushed us. We obeyed. She hung up. We waited as she looked from Herm to me and back to Herm. "The person who does the tours is out for a week."

I started blurting, "I'm sorry. I just figured you could walk in. Like a museum. But I should've checked, I know. I couldn't imagine not having a tour. Why don't they have a tour?"

She nodded but didn't answer and I heard Herm whisper, "Uh-oh." Because Susy Liu Anne was silent, which meant pissed off, and I got to thinking my skin could be like the *plip-plap*ping tape and that if she wanted, she'd start ripping my hide off shred by shred. So I got pissed off that I hadn't called ahead. A complete idiot. God, I'm an idiot sometimes—I know that's what Susy Liu Anne was thinking: *Why the hell didn't he call ahead? Lazy—that's why.*

Calm as ever, she took a sip of her coffee. Mine was churning good in my gut.

"Sel," she said. There was no sweetness in her voice, no anger either. I couldn't even hear her accent. "Do you want to see the clock?"

Instead of thinking about the clock, I got to thinking conspiracy, which I wasn't sure wasn't the real reason I was there. But that got me wondering how many movies are out there where the guy goes off chasing a conspiracy and doesn't have his friend die, car explode and wife leave him. None. So I answered the truth.

"I don't know."

Herm was quick on that, and shrill. "Again! Shit, Sel. Decide something."

"What difference is it going to make, Herm, if we see it or not? What?" It wasn't as if Joalene was going to come crawling back and we'd live happily ever after in a three-bedroom, two-story house with a pool. Just the opposite. "I'll go back to the library and home and sit on my lounger with the dead tree outside. I'll be me, and Waketon will be Waketon."

Herm lost it. "*WHAT THE HELL IS THAT?— 'WAKETON WILL BE WAKETON'?*"

"Nothing's going to change."

Herm shoved himself up from the table. Normally, Susy Liu Anne would've told him to sit down and take it easy, particularly with the people inside staring and the people waiting outside eyeballing us through the window. She didn't though. Just watched all calm and peaceful while Herm rolled on.

"I got soaked because of that windshield, and I'll probably get pneumonia. I might die. That'd be change for you, all right. And you're just goin' to go home and sit on your ass and hide away, you fat piece of shit."

I should have laid back into him, the scrawny asshole yelling at me that way. Again. But I didn't have the strength. And again he was right. I did want to go home and sit on the lounger with a few quarts and let the dust settle into my craw.

So Herm said, "Honey. He's seein' the clock. I don't care what the hell he says."

She smiled big and loving at him, in a way I couldn't remember seeing. "I'll take care of it," she told him.

"Good," he said. "'Cause I gotta pee." He gave me the wave of disgust and headed for the bathroom. Susy Liu Anne watched him leave, then without saying anything, put on her jacket, walked outside and got back on the phone, leaving me alone among the gawkers to ruminate on my procrastination.

A few minutes later Herm returned and sat. His disgust had gone. "Sorry," he said.

"No problem." Because it wasn't a problem—not when he's right.

"But you're goin' to see the clock."

I looked out the window at Susy Liu Anne, gloves on and bundled up, sweet-talking someone on the phone. "Okay," I said.

"You know, though, you're the one with the job."

"But you work from home."

"Some joy that is." He bent his head to his soda and sucked on the straw.

"No boss. No schedule or commute."

"And nothin' in my craw. Except your goddamn clocks. And that's barely a crumb. 'Cause it's yours. Other than that, there ain't been nothin' for years."

"Except the Blue Socks."

Herm snickered and scoffed, "Friggin' Blue Socks."

Trying to be funny, I said, "Blue Socks and diapers."

"Go to hell, Sel." But he wasn't mad. More sad than anything, looking into his soda and circling the straw around the ice cubes.

"A thing's a thing," I said, repeating his words.

"No, Sel. It ain't. We got no kids. Might never have any if things don't change."

"What things?"

"Nothin' things."

"No—what is it?"

"Leave it. I shouldn't've brought it up."

"Sorry." It was my turn to apologize.

"That's all right." His voice turned solemn, as if he'd just seen the Blue Socks give up a nine-run lead in the eighth inning. "Too many babies anyway. Everyone but us. Spewin' 'em out. Buyin' diapers faster than I can make 'em. And now I need a new plant."

"That's good then."

"I hate diapers, Sel. I hate the smell of 'em, the touch of 'em. I even hate pictures of 'em, which is all I see anymore anyways. But I still hate 'em. Jiminy."

Sometimes with your best friends, there's a time to shut yourself up and sit. As long as you're there, it's okay. Around a woman, of course, I'd start asking if she wanted a slice of pizza or say something else stupid that would send her off in a huff. But with Herm, I just knew.

After another five minutes of us sitting and not talking, Susy Liu Anne came back in and stood beside Herm, put her arm on his shoulder and gave him a mischievous grin.

"I knew you could do it," said Herm.

She smiled, and to me specifically said, "All right, boys, it's time to see Time."

19

THE BOWELS OF TIME

I'd expected a big building, at least six stories high with little windows and a big iron gate—something mean-looking, to protect the clock. But where that was supposed to be was a low-slung building with "NIST" on the side in big blue letters. It was concrete, of course, and stone, and police cars were parked near the entrance, but the "Department of Commerce" letters on the front could've been "Boulder High School," and except for all the other low-slung buildings around it, no one would've been surprised. We did get guards and a gate, but even that was more the railroad type than the jail type. It just didn't seem like that big of a deal to me.

"Shoot. We could sneak in if we wanted," Herm said.

"No need for that," said Susy Liu Anne.

Herm parked by the visitors' center, a little one-story

building to the side of the gate. Inside was one of those curved, cubicle-style reception counters, an X-ray machine for walking through, a bunch of office furniture and cabinets, four guards and no visitors but us.

Susy Liu Anne walked to the counter. "I'm Ms. Poderosa," she said.

The guard smiled, as if recognizing her. "It's a pleasure to meet you."

"It's nice to meet you, too."

"You're not what I expected."

"A Mr. Kerquin is expecting us," she said, ignoring the comment.

"Mr. Kerquin is your sponsor?"

"Yes, he is."

"You went to the top, ma'am."

"There's not a problem, is there?"

"No, ma'am," he said. "No problem."

We went through the X-ray, got our pictures taken and badges made while the guards checked the car for bombs and guns and chemical weapons.

A minute later in came this ruffled-up guy with tan skin, brown hair standing up all over, and glasses of course, but broad shoulders. Basically he had the build of a swimmer and the face of a geek.

He said, "Welcome," and smiled big and friendly and went straight for Susy Liu Anne and shook her hand. "Ms. Poderosa. It's very nice to meet you."

"And you as well, Mr. Kerquin."

To Herm and me, he was extra hearty. "I hear you're

here to see the clock."

I didn't much want to answer because I still wasn't so sure, so I waited for Herm to nod and say, "Yep. The big guy is. I'm along for the ride."

"Well, I don't do tours, but I can let you take a quick look."

"Thanks," I said.

"My pleasure. A thousand miles in a day is quite a lot."

I said, "Longer, if you're a Satan follower."

Herm gave me the nail-gun glare, and Kerquin cocked his head but didn't comment. "The clock's in the main building." Which is where he'd come from, so we climbed in the Town Car, nodded to the guards as we drove through the gate, and parked in a director's spot. "I live close, so I walk to work."

"Cool," said Herm.

As we walked to the entrance, Susy Liu Anne slid up beside the research man and thanked him all sweetly for taking the time out of his busy schedule to see us. "You know, there would have been no living with either of them if we didn't at least get to see the clock. I really hope it's not a problem."

"None at all."

Susy Liu Anne took to his side while Herm and I trailed. And I got to thinking about this guy Kerquin, picturing him in high school. He wasn't part of the main crowd, but he probably went to a football party every once in a while and was cheered when he came in and cheered when he chugged, because he swam, and swam well, and probably held a record, or three, national ones of course. That's the kind of geek Kerquin was—the cool one.

He ushered us along the walkway, past a tall, snow-covered pine, into the lobby, up a set of stairs and through double doors. The floor was white mottled tile and the walls cinder block and white except for two stripes, one blue and one red, about halfway up. Herm's and my heels kept squeaking and Susy Liu Anne's clicking, but no one else seemed to walk by. There could've been zombies hiding behind the walls. Herm even whispered it to me once. "Don't touch anything; your skin will rot." It was spooky.

Susy Liu Anne started asking Kerquin about the place—how many people worked there and what they did and where were their offices, which all seemed empty.

"There's an off-site today."

"Everyone?"

"Most. A few are lingering. The addicted ones who can't leave their research."

"That's sad," said Susy Liu Anne.

"That's the hard reality of life as a physicist."

"Well, I think we have a few questions about physics, if you don't mind."

"Shoot."

So Susy Liu Anne turned back to me. "Sel...," she said, prompting me.

I started to speak, slowly, carefully, because I didn't have an interview list of questions or even an outline or anything. I asked him the first one I remembered. "How did you all come up with a second?"

"It's cycles of the cesium atom."

"Who decided how many?"

"Well…" He paused. And then as we wound our way up and down stairwells lined with government-gray sound absorbers and down hallways with pipes and tubes above, Kerquin went on and explained to us the history of the second. I'll summarize as best I can.

First there was the day—sun up, sun down. The cavemen even knew it. But then people like the Babylonians and Egyptians, back in the BCs, started dividing the days into twenty-fourths. And the Babylonians started using sixty, because sixty was big in their counting system, so that's why we got sixty minutes in an hour and sixty seconds in a minute.

The Egyptians wrote a lot of stuff down, about Time and the planets and math and how they all work together. Except a bunch of it got burned in the Crusades, like a whole libraryful, and all the science people had to relearn it all. That's what Kerquin said, at least. But they—the Egyptians—supposedly had the mean month, meaning the average, down pretty close, because they measured around solstices. But with the days getting longer and shorter all year long, figuring out an hour was pretty hard. Sundials and water clocks helped, but it wasn't until the Brits got into it with the grandfather pendulum clock that everyone started trying to track it to the second.

The problem was, they had to get the arm of the pendulum the right length, every time, or the second would be off and then the minutes, and then the hours wouldn't match the sundial out back by the fountain. The Royal Society of London, this club of snobby people, did pretty much all the counting of ticks and comparing and changing pendulums every week or so to try to figure out exactly what a second was. Now, I'm not saying the royals are involved in any sort of Garfield-murdering Time conspiracy. I'm just saying that the Brits were the ones who defined the second as one half swing of a one-meter pendulum on the earth's surface.

"That was the first paradigm shift," Kerquin said. "Taking the second as the basis for Time, rather than the year, changed everything."

But the pendulum had problems, because if it was real cold the arm would shrink and swing fast, and if it was warm the arm would get longer and slow down. So a second was never exactly the same, which meant counting up from something small didn't work, because unless you were exact, the more you counted, the further off you got.

So then, in 1956, they went backwards with the paradigm and redefined the second as a part of the period of the earth's movement; the second became—and this is straight out of one of the science books—1/31,556,925.9747 of the tropical year for 1900 January 0 at 12-hour ephemeris time, which has to do with the whole movement of the stars and the planets and the sun and moon.

"But that's not the end," Kerquin said. "It was about this time—not to make a pun—that the first cesium clock was invented. Much like the one we have here. However, it wasn't until 1967 that the paradigm swung backwards yet again. Rather than divide the year, we defined the second as the duration of 9,192,631,770 periods (he had it memorized) of the radiation corresponding to the transition between the two hyperfine levels of the ground state of the cesium-133 atom."

Brilliant.

Count count count count count.

That's all we're doing. Suns and moons and seasons and swings, only now it's periods of radiation, which I still can't explain very well, even after seeing it and listening and reading some more on it. We're counting. And that paradigm shift we're all talking about really doesn't start at the second anyway; it starts with the cesium atom spitting off a tiny bit of radiation that we, or the physicists actually, count. All the way up to nine trillion and something.

Once again, I was feeling pretty smart. So smart that when we walked into the clock room and Kerquin announced, "Here we are," I found myself smiling.

But not because of the clock. It wasn't impressive at all. For one, it was covered in plastic. And two, it's basically a silver tube about six feet tall. The coolest part was all the mirrors surrounding it, like a hundred or so, that they shoot the lasers off of so that they hit the cesium just right. But the clock was turned off. It only runs a week a month, and then it's only used to set a bunch of other atomic clocks sitting on shelves in another room. They're the ones that really tell time. They're the ones that get beamed out to everywhere.

Susy Liu Anne took a couple of pictures. Herm walked around the contraption, and I just looked at it for a few seconds. Then I asked the guy. I said, "So, Doc, all you're doing is counting something. Right? Just counting something and adding them together and calling it Time."

He smiled. "For our purposes, yes."

"And what are your purposes?"

"We're an organization of standards, Mr. Selraybob. There are many uses for standards of Time. But," he said, "we're not defining Time. We are merely measuring it as accurately and precisely as is possible."

"What do you mean you're not defining it?"

"Every time you move, you move through Time."

"But there is no Time unless something moves. If nothing moved, there wouldn't be Time."

"Time is the continuum through which people and objects move."

"But if nothing moves, there's no continuum, because you can't count."

Mr. Kerquin had been a pleasant guy all in all and wasn't much for arguing. He told me, "I understand your point. It's a theory. You aren't the first one."

"I'm not?"

"You're not."

I was actually shocked to hear it, or at least for him to say it. I knew other people thought about Time my way, at least a few, like the female fixer, but since it was so simple, it only made sense that the physicists would have changed something, agreed that Time's a count, and if there's nothing to count, not even an atom, then there's no Time. Maybe that's what they were hiding. So conspiracy seeped out of my craw and onto my tongue and I asked about Garfield. I said, "What happened to Garfield?"

Kerquin took a lean back—not a big one, but enough to tell I'd surprised him. At least that's what Susy Liu Anne told me later. And he said, "You mean, the former president Garfield?"

"Yeah," I said. "What happened to him?"

"What makes you ask?"

"I heard some talk back home."

"Conspiracy talk?"

"Kind of."

He laughed. "It's all over the Internet, Mr. Selraybob. Garfield's the latest. According to the Assassinationists, as they're known here, we've been holding the secret of Time hostage here for over fifty years. It's somewhere beneath the clock, in a secret room with hidden doors. It'll evaporate the universe if it gets out."

"But the secret is that there is no Time."

With that, he paused, took a deep breath and looked straight at Susy Liu Anne. "Where are you from?"

"Waketon, Missouri."

He grinned and nodded. "Ah, Waketon. That seems to be the center of the movement."

"We're the center?" I said.

And Herm chimed in: "You mean, Waketon, hellhole, Missouri is where all of this crap started?" And without waiting for an answer, he asked me, "Did you hear that,

Sel? The center."

"I heard," I said. But I was too formal and too stiff, and Herm saw it plain as day.

"Shit! You knew about this conspiracy crap, didn't you?"

"Herm! Sel didn't know anything." Susy Liu Anne whacked his arm, and he cringed, and she asked me sweetly, "Did you, Sel?"

"I heard talk."

"You heard talk?" said Herm.

"At the library."

"People don't talk at the library."

"You work at the library?" That was Kerquin.

"Yeah," I said. "So what?" They were all attacking me.

"You don't look like a librarian, Mr. Selraybob. A shining example that you can never tell a book by its cover."

"Yeah. 'Cause I always thought Sel had some sense."

I told them all, "I'm not saying I believed it."

"You're not sayin' you didn't."

Susy Liu Anne stepped between Herm and me to calm us down. "I'm sure Sel was only humoring the idea."

Kerquin chuckled. "It's a funny thing, these conspiracies."

"Yes it is," added Susy Liu Anne.

"Real funny," said Herm, letting us all know it wasn't anymore.

"Well then…" Kerquin's voice was extra cheery, and he put on a grin and held his arms wide like a bartender at 2:00 a.m. "Take a last look. I have work to attend to."

But just as we were ready to step back out into the hallway with the red and blue stripes, Susy Liu Anne gave a long stroke to Kerquin's arm and asked, "And where are you from, Mr. Kerquin?"

I'm sure not an expert, but he didn't seem all excited to answer. Unfortunately for him, for even the most stubborn, it's hard not to spill when Susy Liu Anne starts sweet-talking you and petting your arm.

"Why do you ask?"

"You seem like an island guy," she said.

"So you've read my bio?"

"No. You have that island air about you. As if the world around you liked the calm. It's sweet."

"I'm from Maui."

"No shit?" I blurted. "You're really from Hawaii?"

"Yes."

"You know any Hamayans?"

He gave me that curious look with the crooked smile, the kind that makes you wonder what side of the truth the next words will come from. "What's a Hamayan?" he asked.

"Half Hawaiian, half Mayan. You don't know?"

He ignored the question. "And they're in Waketon?"

"A couple of them."

Mr. Kerquin was getting tired of conspiracy jawing and he went all peace-loving and said, "Look. This is a typical Internet conspiracy theory. They happen all of the time. For a while, a group insisted that our atomic clock was a doomsday device counting down to the end of the time. That one was out of Condon, Montana. Population six hundred."

So Herm asked, "Well, is it?"

Kerquin laughed again. "We'd have died at the turn of the century."

"You hear that, Sel? They're typical Waketon quacks."

Kerquin put his arm on Herm's shoulder all buddy-buddy but talked at me. "You have to step lightly with those Time folks. They want to uproot the world, undo Einstein."

And then I said again, "But Time really is just a count."

Kerquin threw out a quick, frustrated, "Huch."

"And there is no space-time. It's made up."

"Be careful, Selraybob. There's passion, and then there's Time passion. You can get yourself so enthralled that you never find your way back."

I wasn't sure if that was a bad idea or not—getting lost far away from the lounger. Which is where I was—far away. But like I said, I wasn't sure.

"I was just asking," I said.

"I realize that."

I was also thinking he was too tall to be Hamayan, and didn't have the nose or the forehead. So maybe that was the Mayan side. Or maybe it didn't mean anything. Maybe I was a quack. Because he was really smart—I could tell—and this Hawking guy and a bunch of other geniuses think Time's a Big Deal. So maybe it is. HUGE. It's got to be. If anyone's a quack, it's the shop-watcher guy and me for listening.

Except, three steps after heading down the hall, I

noticed a display I'd missed on the way in. Right across from the clock room, behind glass and on shelves, were three round-and-round clocks and an hourglass and something like a satellite with panels on the side. In the middle of the display were three typed signs. The first was the only one I read before Kerquin, with his arms still wide, ushered us down the hallway. But the words stuck.

Time is defined as the accumulation of atomic seconds beginning 0000 Hours UT(earth time) 1 January, 1958.

It wasn't until we stepped back into the atrium that I spoke, and then it was only to shake Kerquin's hand and tell him, "Thank you for the tour." It was all very formal for us. We said our goodbyes. He told us he hoped we enjoyed it, wished us a good trip back, and reminded us how ridiculous some conspiracies can be.

That's when the front desk guard appeared to escort us back to our car. As we were walking back to the car with the guard, this tall guy with dark sunglasses, government-gray hair, a government-gray suit, a matching shirt, and skin almost as gray walked past and headed in.

I looked back through the window and saw Kerquin waiting inside. A few seconds later I glanced again, and they were together, talking and looking out at us. I waved. Kerquin nodded. The gray man glared.

So I asked the guard who the man was.

"Never seen him before."

"Never?"

"No, sir."

It was Herm who said, "I think he's a spy."

Susy Liu Anne slapped his shoulder. "Herm!"

"What?"

"Quiet."

Herm looked sincerely hurt as we walked back to the car and headed out. The gate guard said his goodbye to Ms. Poderosa and we drove out through the gate and onto Broadway. I spent the drive back to the hotel ruminating as best I could on the sign behind the glass and why, if it was practically shouting into the clock room, didn't Kerquin just come out and say "Time is a count." You can't accumulate without counting. That's all accumulating is— sticking a bunch of crap in a line and then counting up what you got.

And why was he waiting for the government gray man? And why'd they stare at us like we were bombers? We weren't bombers. I just wanted to see the bloody clock.

We were sitting downstairs at the Corner Bar, Susy Liu Anne between us. "What a good trip," she said, petting my arm the way she'd petted Kerquin's. "I'm so glad we saw the clock."

I sipped my beer, not too excited about the drive out and drive here just to find out that Time was a count and that everyone already knew.

So I asked them, "Did you guys see the sign?"

"What sign?"

"The Time definition sign."

"There was a Time definition?"

"It's an accumulation of seconds."

Susy Liu Anne let her hand rest on my arm. "That means you were right, Sel."

"I know." But for some reason being right wasn't making me feel all vindicated and uppity. Instead I had the dull ache from the dull question that never makes anyone feel good unless there's a good answer, which there wasn't—what's it matter?

Herm had asked it before. Joalene had too, basically. Only Susy Liu Anne hadn't asked it. But she's an Asian Southerner with a Mexican last name, and all she'd been trying to do was perk me up and get me out of the house. Shit. What a hell of a winter, and all it comes down to is a silver tube and a bunch of mirrors. And a Hamayan and a man with a government-gray suit.

Susy Liu Anne turned to face me straight on. "He was lying."

Herm answered first. "I told you he was a spy."

She went on. "He'd heard of the Hamayans. I think he even knew the ones in Waketon."

Then Herm again, excited: "I knew something was up!"

"Something sure is," she said. "You can never take the surface as it appears. Mr. Kerquin said it himself."

Herm leaned into Susy Liu Anne, put his arm over her shoulder and said, "That's why they keep everything gray."

"Right, honey!" She took her hand from my arm and gave Herm a big, excited pat. "Gray obscures everything. You have to look underneath, at what he didn't say and what he didn't show us. What didn't he show us, Sel?"

"When she's coming back."

Herm shouted, enough to get the whole bar staring. *"Joalene? You're still talking about Joalene?"*

To Susy Liu Anne I asked, "She's happier in her new life, isn't she?"

"You're a good man, sweetheart. You never know."

"Or maybe you do."

With that I said goodnight and headed upstairs to the room, sat on the bed and stared at the gray TV screen not on and wondered why I'd made the trip all the way to a highfalutin hotel with a stained-glass ceiling and swirly wallpaper—as the third wheel. Was it to see the clock? Chase a conspiracy? Or to figure this whole time thing out, become a professor at SEMO, ride a bike to work?

No. I wasn't going to be a professor. Didn't want to admit it, but I knew all along—I hadn't even been to college. And that's who she was probably with—some professor guy with little glasses. Kind of like Kerquin, but with short hair.

There's something about being alone in an old hotel with friends downstairs probably smooching that makes you notice you're alone. So I flipped on the TV. A beautiful couple was kissing in some reality show, so I switched the channel. A sex therapist jabbered about intimacy in the bedroom. I flipped it off and called Joalene. She didn't answer. I didn't leave a message. I flipped the TV back on. *The Princess Bride*—the most romantic movie ever. "As you wish," the pirate's yelling to her as he's rolling down the hill. And the beautiful heroine leaps and tumbles down after him, realizing she'd found true love again after five long, horrible years.

I flipped it off, emptied the last half of my Busch in three gulps, put on my coat and headed downstairs for more beer. Gallons more.

20

DANGLING

Lovey-dovey romance is even worse live than on TV, so when I saw Herm and Susy Liu Anne still at the bar, talking close and holding hands, I hustled out the side exit. I'd gone a good mile when the snow started. Not heavy, but enough to wet my hair, which made me even colder. So I ducked into a liquor mart called the Liquormart, thinking I was going to get warm with another quart. But just inside I saw bins full of those mini bottles of liquor, like fifty of them—tequila, bourbon, vodka—everything. I decided I wanted something that burned, since it was cold out, and bought a few maximum-proof Southern Comforts and a couple tequilas and chugged one right outside of the store. Burned my throat and my chest and my stomach and every goddamn thing in my body except the part that made me think about Joalene. That part seemed to crank along just fine, not flinching or twisting or flushing its way out—just telling me she's out with some degreed guy and laughing and touching his arm and flipping her hair at every little fucking nibble of wit.

I left the parking lot and went walking through the cold and around the block and looked up into the falling snow and wondered what was going on up there in the stars behind and how they all moved and why we moved, since that's how we know a day's a day in the first place, and a year a year and that a day's changing. I remembered that from one of my books, that our day's getting longer because the earth is slowing down. But I didn't know if that meant the year was getting longer or if there'd just be fewer days.

Shit, Sel. What's it matter?

So I opened a Southern Comfort and sat on a curb in an alley and sipped. No matter how much sugar they put in bourbon, if it's a hundred proof, it burns. It burned as bad as the tequila.

A couple gulps and another mini later, my head got heavy and my chest woozy. I'd been used to three quarts a day for years, four quarts there for a while, but they were always spread out. Southern Comfort hadn't gone down my gullet since high school, watching Joalene out dancing while I was against the wall with the rest of the linemen getting hammered and wishing we were svelte and charming and played quarterback. Every fucking one of us wished we'd played quarterback. That son of a bitch Reggie had the life. That bastard.

I found myself getting pissed, really pissed, and I didn't

like it. I don't get pissed off—at least not at someone else. Except maybe the Round Mound of Time Fixing. And maybe Mr. Shaved Calves. Besides them, it'd been a long time. Really. So I finished off the last tequila in one gulp, then pushed myself up, and wobbled, and sat myself right back down. "Whoa," I remember saying, needing an arm to brace myself. To ease the spin, I put my head between my knees. It didn't work. I puked. Twice. The second one was a multiheave vomit that left my stomach muscles aching.

The cold helped, and the accumulating snow, so after a few minutes of deep breaths, I tried again to stand and walk, and this time, after a few wobbles and a stumble, I succeeded. I trudged back to the hotel and got myself back in bed with a couple of glasses of water. I turned on the TV and turned it off and wondered why people got mad and what good it did and if someone could actually punch someone. I hadn't. Not even in high school or in a game. I might've knocked linebackers on their asses, but in a fight I was the one to break things up, not bash noses. Which made me feel real stupid remembering how I was going to break the Time fixer's knees.

I woke up before the sun and without even showering knocked on Herm's room, woke them up and asked for the car key. "I'm going to start packing," I told him. What I wanted was a quart. Herm got me the key.

"We're going back to sleep."

Which was perfect. I headed straight down, brushed the couple inches of snow from the trunk, took out a quart, and leaned against the car and downed a few swigs. After about four gulps my stomach gurgled. Bile started to rise. My mouth got that sour taste again that was a prelude to a puke. So I threw the rest in the trash. Really. It was basically full. Then, not knowing exactly what I wanted to do, I jumped in the Town Car and took it out for a spin. I didn't feel like breakfast, and I didn't feel like seeing the city or driving around the mall, and even though the roads were clear, I figured if I went up to the mountains, I'd get stuck needing chains. So when I saw a sign for the Boulder Reservoir I headed that way, to see the ice at sunrise.

I drove by the empty check-in booth and out to the building by the shore and parked. There was no one there on a Tuesday morning in February, so I got out and walked up to the building and looked out from the deck at the snow-covered lake. Not much of a reflection, even with the sun up, but the mountains were like shining towers in the distance. Not as majestic as the roaring Mississippi, but I could figure why people liked them.

Below was a small sandy beach and an open pool in the ice. Off to my side, leaning against a rail was a leftover sign from some Polar Plunge for Special Olympics. *Shit*, I thought. *A bunch of granolas jumping in the water.* But after that thought, came: *Tougher than you are, big guy. Can't stand the cold. Want to sit your ass on the lounger.* It was a stream of badgering for wasting months thinking about Time. So after a disgusted pat on my gut, I headed for the steps and down to the beach and stood looking at the water and around for people. It was quiet still, that early, with the sun just starting to shine off the little spot of water.

There are times, and I was having a run of them, that you do something you don't really want to do, and have no good reason to do, but you do it anyway. I had no intention when I made the turn to the reservoir of jumping in. It wasn't in my head when I passed the booth, and it wasn't even in my head when I'd walked down to the sand. It didn't get into my head until I pictured a gaggle of granola-eating college pukes splashing around that I took off my jacket and decided I was sure as shit tougher than they were. They probably wore wet suits anyway. So within a minute my shirt was off and my pants, and I was down to my boxers. But even those were cheating, so I stripped naked and stood at the beach and looked at the ice. I found myself grinning. "All right, Sel. Time to swim." I even laughed at the words. Then I dug my toes into the sand and ran with my arms flailing like a kid's and bashed into the water. Losing my breath didn't stop me. I kept plowing through, up to my waist, until finally, with another grin and another breath, I dove underneath. A few seconds later I came up with a big old *Aaaharrrr* kind of mountain-man yell. Just a few feet behind me was the ice edge, so figuring I was a mountain man, I growled and lunged and banged my fists into the ice like I was taking down a mountain lion. With another growl and head dunk and with a chunk of ice held over my head like a trophy, I stomped out of the water and back onto the beach.

That's when the cold hit. Every little bit—from the dangling parts in front to my hand holding the ice, which I dropped, to my feet—everything burned from the cold. I was half expecting icicles to start forming on the dripping parts. And I was towel-less, and didn't have a change of clothes, and didn't want to put on the ones I had, because they'd get wet and keep me wet and cold, and if I wasn't careful, I'd probably freeze my toes off while I was trying to pull everything on. So I grabbed up my clothes and started running for the Town Car, straight past a group of winter walkers with hiking poles and boots. They waved, grinned, nodded, and stared. One asked, "How's the water?"

I grinned at the group. "Refreshing," I said, and kept running to the car.

21

THE COMING
OF THE FEMALE FIXER

I went back to work, making sure the books were nice and neat and according to library code. Afternoons I ran the hill with Carl. At night I did push-ups and in the morning sit-ups. Now and then I'd pet the cur dog and order a chicken and make it last two dinners and a breakfast. I even bought fruit once—apples. Time popped into my acorn a few times, but I'd just ask myself, *What's it matter?*, and answer, *It doesn't*, then go back to whatever I'd been doing. It was a good two weeks—I was slimming down still, paying my bills, keeping oil in the Corvair and making my way like everyone else in Waketon—steady and smooth and regular. The way life's supposed to be. Regular. I was actually restacking misplaced books and telling myself exactly that—*You're a regular guy, Sel. Regular as the river*—when in walked the female clock fixer.

She didn't notice me at first, but I noticed her as she passed a gap two aisles away in this loose black dress that matched her hair. My acorn filled with memories of the smile and the joy of meeting at her clock shop and going all unsettled in the stomach and throat and joints. It happened again right there, with just a glance. So I followed her, peering between the books as I went, and going through my head what it was she was searching for and what she was reading, since she wasn't in the clock section, the 680s, or the Time section, which is spread around the 500s science stuff; she was in the 900s, the history section. I wasn't sure what she was doing there or what she needed, and it was my job to serve the customers. As regular as I could, I tucked my shirt and pulled my sagging pants up, smoothed everything down and walked out of my aisle and around to the aisle of the female fixer. She was much taller than I'd pictured back in her clock shop, with shinier hair too, and a hell of a lot more intimidating once the desk wasn't between us. I was out, exposed, a few feet from the source of all the world's butterflies.

She glanced back and saw me and I almost upchucked right then.

But I didn't, because it was my job to help people. That's what I told myself. *It's your job, Selraybob. Help the lady.* So I swallowed my gag and said, "Can I help you?"

"Oh," she said. "Hello." She was smiling, but backing up the way they do when you catch them stalker-like by surprise. So I told her right away that I worked there now, and that it was my job to help and if there was anything she wanted—I mean, I was blurting, *blah blah blah blah*—but if there was anything she wanted about Time or clocks or some sort of new physics book that might have come out, to let me know.

"Well...," she said in that cocked-head way that people get when they're thinking.

So real fast I said, "I can order more books if you don't see what you want."

"No no. No. I'm okay. I'm only browsing." She walked around me, skimming my shirt, and asked me how my own Time thinking was going and if I'd come up with any more theories. She was totally nonchalant when she said it. And that's when I noticed we were in the 972s, the Central America section. I looked around and saw a Mayan book and remembered the calendar bit. So I told her how I'd been reading about the calendar mostly, and the history, and about the Mayan calendar too, and how it's totally different.

"Thirteen," I said. "It's a big number to the Mayans. An important one, I mean. Not bad luck or anything. It's like they have a thirteen-day week." Which is all I really remembered about the whole thing.

She stared for a few seconds. "The Mayans," she said. "Not the Aztecs?"

"I don't remember much about the Aztecs."

She nodded and looked away and around, as if I'd bored her completely. As if I'd been talking about the dust mites or maybe even the great left tackles in the history of the NFL. Something like that would've bored any woman.

She said, "It's all mythology anyway."

"Yeah," I said. "It's all fake."

She walked on with this "I'm so superior" attitude that got me going in a way I can't really talk about and didn't want to show. It was like in high school, seeing Joalene do a split-leg jump in her pleated skirt with the yellow undies. That's how the female fixer's "I'm so cool" spin and saunter got to me. It was real bad.

At the end of the aisle she stopped. "Where are the clock books?" she asked.

"Aisle four."

She turned the corner and I glanced around to see if anyone else needed any special help, but it was two-thirty, a half hour before the after-school crowd and Carl. So I followed. She said, "Time is a count, you say?"

"Doesn't mean much though, when you think about it."

"I wouldn't say that." She didn't look at me much, not when she talked, and not when she listened either. Not at all actually, except when I'd mentioned the Mayans, and then only for a second. "Time can mean more than a count." Then quickly: "That's what they say."

"It just seems like a count," I said.

"What about relativity?"

"That Hawking thing?"

Now, I don't believe in any of that ESP crap, but I swear, right while she was snickering, I heard in her voice, plain as day, *Oh, you poor boy,* right before she said out loud—and this I know she said—"That Einstein thing."

"Oh, yeah. Einstein. The German guy."

She turned into the clock aisle. "Yes," she said. "The German." Then she smiled big and turned and glanced down at my name tag. "Selraybob?"

"Yes."

"That's your name?"

"Yes."

"No last name?"

"Not really. And most people I know call me Sel anyway."

"Well then, Sel, thank you."

It was all very pleasant and proper. "You're welcome," I said.

"It was nice seeing you again."

"If you need anything…"

"I know where you work."

"And I know where you work," I said.

"Yes," she said, "you do," and turned away and walked down the next aisle and looked at the books, pulled one out and began to read.

I stood for a second, waiting for her to look up again. She didn't. So I headed back to the desk.

My craw, of course, was full again of new Time things, like the female fixer and clock shops and Mayans and thirteen and what was a clock fixer doing looking at the South American history? And what about the Aztecs? And do I have ESP? And finally, or am I just being an idiot again? That was the big one, which was good, because ten minutes later, even before the fixer in the black dress had left, Carl showed up, and we headed out to the hill and started our running and squats and left-tackle moves.

Second time up the hill, standing on top and looking down at us, was the female fixer.

"You have a son?" she said.

"No," I said. "We're just getting ourselves in shape."

Right off, Carl introduced himself and stuck out his hand. "I'm Carl," he said.

"Nice to meet you, Carl." And she bent and shook.

"What's your name?"

"Sophia," she told him.

Carl told her, "I've lost eight pounds."

Sophia smiled. "Eight pounds. That's good."

And all the sudden she was smiling in a way you knew was a smile and not just a face. Which, once I saw the difference in the same person, I realized that a face is what she'd been making in the library.

Then Carl looked up to me. "He's on break."

I pulled up my sagging pants. "They're loose," I said.

"Oh. You've been losing, too?"

"Some," I said.

Carl said, "But they're going to be looser, too." I'd never seen the kid talk so much. "But my sleeves will be tighter. I've been doing push-ups." I wanted to tell the kid to man up already and stop floundering after her like a guppy.

But then I added, "I'm kind of a mentor." And I felt like an idiot. Because once you call yourself someone's mentor, you become a prick. You really do. Like you're all cool all the sudden. Sophia noticed and Carl noticed, and I was ready for me to head back inside, and so was Sophia. Carl decided he was going to do another hill. But before he went back down, he said, "Selraybob was a tackle. They won state."

Sophia nodded, and her smile became a face and she said, "You must have been good."

"That was a long time ago."

"Oh," she said.

"Yeah."

"Well…"

I said, "Did you believe the world was going to end in 2012?"

She was surprised, and it wasn't just a face. It was pure surprise. She was quick to pull it in, but I'd said something that got her going. So she looked down at Carl and put her smile back on and then to me asked, "Now why would I believe something like that?"

Because I'd remembered all the sudden that 2012 was big for them, so I blurted it out, hoping, I think, that she wouldn't leave. "The Mayan thing. It was big news."

"Did you believe it?"

"I'm just now learning."

Carl came running up, barely huffing, the freshest I'd ever seen the kid after a hill. He told her, "You should see the books he reads. He's way smart."

I grinned.

She said, "I'm sure he is."

"I'm not."

"He is."

To shut Carl up I asked what time it was. He looked at

his watch. "We got a few minutes."

Sophia said, "And I have a few things to take care of."

Then Carl: "He's got to do another hill."

I patted the kid on the back. "One more. Before break's done."

"And before the world explodes," Carl said as he headed down.

"That already passed," I told him.

"So you think we're safe?" she asked.

"Well, yeah. Of course."

Right then, Carl yelled, "You coming?"

I yelled, "Hold on." And to Sophia, softly: "I got to go."

She chuckled. "Me too," she said. "Enjoy your hill."

I shook my head and chuckled along. "He wears me out." And I headed down.

The next day she was back standing at the top of the hill, waiting for Carl and me to climb.

"You doing hills with us?" Carl asked her.

"No no." And her voice was lighter than I'd remembered. Happy. But with her I wasn't sure how close her Face was, if it was poised to come out and phony up. And turn me on. Because I'd seen her without it. It's the seeing someone natural and hot, then having it go into hiding for a while that gets you going. Or me going. Sad as that may sound.

I asked her, "Are you heading in?" Meaning the library.

"I am," she said.

I asked Carl if we were done, and he held up his index

finger. "All right," I said, with a big old puff of air. And to Sophia: "We'll be in in a minute."

"I'll wait."

"Yeah?" That was cool.

"Yes," she said.

"It's cold."

"I like the cold."

"Okay," I said, and practically pushed Carl down the hill. "Let's go, guy. This one's for speed."

Carl walked between us, talking me up, telling Sophia how I'd been helping him with his algebra—which, according to him, I was able to figure out in no time—and how I was getting so fit and how coming to the library isn't so dorky now that I was there. "You know, they even have CDs in here. You can listen for free."

"Not when you're studying," I told him.

I sounded very adult.

"I don't even hate studying anymore. It's still for dweebs, real studying is, but it's okay with Selraybob. I mean, it's not like I get all A's or anything."

Sophia told him, "You know, I have a PhD."

I said, "Oh."

And Carl said, "You been to school a lot. That's what that means."

"I like to learn," she told him. Her voice was as smooth as ever, but softer when she spoke to Carl. It was almost as if she'd been around kids before, regularly, and had been a teacher.

So I asked her, "What did you study?"

"Orbital mechanics."

I couldn't even say "Oh."

Since I'd gone quiet, Carl shared a little fact. "Mr. Sel worked landscape so his girlfriend could go to college."

"Hey," I told him. "None of that."

Carl kept right on spilling. "Right here in Waketon. She went to SEMO. She was a cheerleader."

"Well," said Sophia. "We don't all have the opportunities that I had. I was lucky."

Carl asked, "You had a boyfriend pay?"

"I had a trust."

I near choked on my own vomit. I mean, Jesus Christ. A trust fundee with a PhD in orbital mechanics, and a figure to make Joalene, even at her trimmest, ready to shout, "Anorexic!" Which Sophia's was not. Not at all. Just nice.

We walked inside and everyone got silent. Carl went to his books and I stopped at my desk while Sophia headed for the Mayan section, most of which I'd checked out for myself the day before but hadn't read. Because I sure as hell hadn't planned on her coming back and stepping up to the desk looking for them. Which she did, a minute later.

In and extra soft, almost sultry library voice, she looked down at me and asked, "Has someone been in recently, to the history section?"

I felt small in my chair, and told myself to *Man Up. Get Tall.* I stood. Too fast, of course. I banged my knee, and grimaced.

"You okay?"

I forced a smile. "Good. Yeah. Just a bump."

She smiled back, waiting for an answer.

"What kind of someone?" I said.

"No special kind."

"Like fixers?" I asked.

"Fixers?"

"Time fixers. I mean clock fixers. Repairers. Like you." I was sputtering. "But not like you. Different."

"I see." She nodded. I felt like I was being interviewed. "Have any been any in?"

"The dark twins. The ones with the shops that aren't much alike at all."

"The brooding ones, with black hair and blacker eyes."

"The Hamayans," I said. "Yeah."

"You know them?"

"Not really," I answered. "They seemed kind of suspicious. Probably because the world didn't end, or are they always that way?"

"They're nice, once you get to know them."

"They sure made the watcher nervous—the guy who watches for the big fixer across from the Steak 'n Shake."

"You certainly did make the rounds."

"Heck," I said. "I even went to Colorado. Met this guy named Kerquin."

This time she was shocked. And even though she pulled it back fast, a little still lingered when she asked, "You met Kerquin?"

I was feeling cocky with her surprise, and I puffed up and told her, "Yeah. He told me about the Internet hoax.

Thought it was funny. We sure got a few quacks in Waketon…according to him."

"There are quacks everywhere." She stepped sideways, interview over, and started slinking away.

I blurted, "What books are you looking for?"

She barely looked back. "The twins probably took them."

"You mean the Mayan books?"

She stopped. "Yes."

"No. They're at home."

"At your home?" She flitted her hair and cocked her head all coy.

"They were never checked out."

"Hmm." She put one hand on a hip, which pulled her jacket open and exposed a sweater-covered breast and low-waisted jeans, not at all what I pictured for an astrophysics doctorate. So, with my cockiness puffed into my chest as big as ever and my idiocy blocker again turned into a greased-up, gaping hole of *Come on through,* I spat out, "How about a review? Where the books are. At my house."

"That would be nice," she answered.

Oh shit. She's really coming. My stomach churned.

Her eyes crinkled with a smile. "I'll be gone a few days. Is Sunday good?"

"Okay," I grunted.

"Good." She leaned towards me, and I swear her lips were puckered and she was about to give me a cheek peck. "Noon?"

The last wisps of cockiness dropped straight to my acid-filled belly. If I'd opened my mouth she'd smell the bile, so I turned my head and mumbled, "Uh. Yeah. Noon."

She pulled back, said, "Wonderful. See you then," and whisked around and strode away.

And I sprinted to the restroom to vomit.

22

THE SEDUCTIVE EFFECTS OF TIME
THEORY

All I was thinking really, when I invited her, was about Time, and how stupid I was and how smart she was and pretty. I wasn't thinking sex at all. Yes, she'd got me going, but that's different. I was in the library, with kids around. And it had been so long since I'd had sex—well over a year, and even longer since I'd felt like anything but a blundering fool—that I wasn't even sure I wanted it anymore.

Until Sunday morning, three days later, when Sophia pulled up along the curb and walked across the yard with this ankle-length coat and big sway. That was the prelude. When she swooshed by me with a sultry, "Hello, Selraybob"—that got things stirring. But as soon as she crossed under the doorway and into the house—that's when I started thinking about her legs twisted through mine and our chests pressed together and her heart beating and her lips wet from her tongue that had been flicking out slowly, as if to taste the salt of my neck that she was about to kiss, any second, while she stretched her arm over my shoulder and reached down my back.

I practically chased her inside.

"So," she said, "you've got the Mayan books?"

"Uh-huh."

"They're fascinating, I would imagine. How do you find them?" And as she was talking, she was giving the place the 360, vertical, forward, backward, and every-way scan. I even saw her check the ceiling, which I realized was a blend of white and brown and scuz that in this spot above the lounger kind of looked like a pair of breasts, which I wish I wouldn't have noticed, seeing as Sophia's jacket was open and loose but her sweater wasn't, and she was nowhere near flat. "Do you find them tedious, or are you just browsing?"

"I haven't gotten into them yet," I said.

"So were they meant to be a lure?" That's when she turned to me and swayed her hips, and that's when I pictured her sweater off and started blabbing.

"No no. I was just curious. Just wondering. I've been reading Time stuff, but not Mayan stuff, at least not something all about the Mayans."

"You knew about thirteen and 2012."

"That was from another book, just a section. And I don't remember anything else. The numbers got stuck, I guess."

"So you're a numbers guy." She smiled, and I tried to

figure out which side of real her face was on. Because the thought of it being fake again was shutting me down. Even if that stuck up and snotty thing gets you going at first, you don't want to get naked with it.

"Is it cold in here?" I said. "I'm a little cold."

"I'm okay."

"I'm going to turn up the heat, if that's all right."

"Sure."

Then I rushed to the back to flip up the heat to eighty-five and rushed back and blabbered away. "It'll be warmer soon. It works real good. You want tea? I'll make some tea. Or coffee. I know how to make coffee now."

"No thanks."

"You want to see the books? They're by the lounger." I rushed to pick them up and show them to her. I picked up a couple of the calendar ones too, since I had the beer table loaded up with them. "This one talks about the earth rotating. And this other one about Easter. And like I said, I haven't read the Mayan ones yet."

She pulled her jacket tight and wrapped her arms across her waist and looked at me politely and at the books and then down to the table at my paper-bag-wrapped *Dictionary of Science*.

"Coffee would be good," she said.

"Yeah?"

"Just a cup."

So I put the books down and rushed around Sophia and into the kitchen and scooped some coffee into the coffee machine, poured in water and turned it on and then ran the six steps back to the living room where she was standing by the lounger and looking down at the Mayan covers and at the backs at the authors. Right as I got close, she turned, and her jacket swept behind her like a gown. She was all the sudden standing in front of me, with her neck stretched long and her pointy little chin jutting out below this—I swear—sultry, lip-only smile. Incredible. I couldn't help but stare. And I did so long that her smile broke into a full-face grin and she turned away and picked up a Mayan book. "How many of these do you have?"

"That's all I got here. I don't know how many we have at the library. I can check if you want. And I can order more. I can find almost anything, if it's in print. And even if it's not, I could probably find it. Is there one that you want?" I finished out of breath.

"No no," she said. "I'm just wondering."

Then I remembered. "Oh. The coffee."

"It smells great."

"It's Cajun, so it's strong. If that's okay." And I rushed into the kitchen.

"It won't hurt. I've got some things to do later."

"Yeah," I said. "So do I." Like more hills. And more push-ups. And maybe even some sit-ups. Because there she was, thin and nice and MIT, and there I was, the left tackle with nine-push-up arms and a gut that not too much earlier touched the ground before I even got my elbows bent. I'd been a teeter-totter almost doing push-ups. So I stood by the coffeepot, listening to the water gurgling up and feeling the steam on my chin. "It's not done yet," I said, like she wouldn't know herself.

"That's all right." She put the book down and opened up my *Dictionary of Science* on the table and asked, "Do you have any Baileys?"

Not even thinking that the sun was hardly up and that I'd hardly slept from all the previsit worrying, I ran to the pantry, where Joalene kept the liquor. "Tequila. No Baileys."

"Any Jack Daniel's?"

"We got Jim Beam."

"That'll do."

"In the coffee?"

"Oh no. On the side. I don't like to mix the flavors."

I pulled out the fifth of Beam. She leaned a shoulder against the wall, one hand down along the thigh of her jeans, and asked me, "How many guys do you think come into the shop and ask about Time?"

"I don't know. A few I guess."

"One."

"Oh."

She kept browsing through the Mayan books and talking while I headed from the kitchen with the coffee. "So you think you have a new theory of Time?"

"Not really," I told her.

"Well, if it's not a theory, what is it?"

"It's just not new. That's what I'm saying. It's like the Greeks. They knew the earth rotated around the sun almost two thousand years ago. And then the Crusaders burned the libraries and almost burned Copernicus like fifteen hundred years later." I handed her the cup of coffee. "That's all I'm saying." The glasses were in the back cupboard and I hurried back and pulled two down. "You want ice?"

"I prefer shots."

"Straight bourbon?"

"Yes." She sipped her coffee. "And you think it's important that people think this way?"

I answered, "No." Because I didn't. "I just had it stuck in my craw and couldn't get it out. Don't ask me why you got to figure stuff out when it gets stuck in your craw. Why'd they care when they figured stuff out?" I pointed at the books. "Who cares if the earth rotates around the sun or the moon or whatever? It got stuck in their craws."

"They hurt a lot of people because of their craws."

I handed her the shot of Beam and asked her, "How?"

"When you fight the system, people get hurt."

"I don't want to fight anything. I just guess I like my craw full."

I swear I saw her squeeze a smile in, one of those that wasn't planned but that the eyes give away. The "like" kind, if I could've believed it.

She noticed my empty hands. "Aren't you doing one?"

"Beer's much better for me."

"Well, you're drinking with me, and I'm not drinking beer." And then came the happy command. "So man up and have a shot. It'll put some warmth into you."

I rushed back to the kitchen and poured myself one then rushed back.

"To Time," she said, and raised her glass.

"To Time," I said. "Cheers." And we clinked glasses and shot our Beam, and she chased it with black coffee and I with a cough and watery eyes and a bad memory of a Colorado curb. "I told you, I'm not a shooter."

"I can see that," she said, and swirled away. She strode towards the books and settled herself on the lounger, stretched her legs out and wiped her hair back from her face. "Bourbon helps clear my head for some good mental stimulation." I was staring again. I couldn't stop. She was in my chair. It wasn't a pretty chair either, and even though I'd cleaned it, I hadn't de-stained. The brown had old beer smudges in it, and some pizza-grease marks. "Time can be stimulating, don't you think?" And her voice kept that smoothness and easy flow, as if she were dancing some sort of classical thing.

Mine didn't. I said, "Yeah," practically grunting. And staring. Like an idiot.

"Sit," she said.

I hesitated.

She scanned the room. "Oh. I'm in your chair."

"No no. That's okay. I'll sit over here." Not on Joalene's chair but by the TV, on the wooden chair that used to go with the dining table I'd broken years before and never fixed.

Sophia set her coffee down and stood. "You sit. I'll find a spot once you're comfortable."

"I'm okay, really. It's fine." But she was already standing at my side, shoulder touching shoulder.

"I'm warming up," she said, and pulled her jacket off her shoulders and stretched her neck long, like a ballet dancer. The coffee was still in my hand while she laid her jacket over Joalene's faded chair and leaned towards me. For the first time I caught a whiff of perfume, soft and feminine. Quietly she said, "Please, Selraybob. Sit."

That's when—I swear—the wind picked up and began blowing through the bare limbs that started scratching against the window.

She didn't seem to notice and leaned in again and said again, "Sit," except this time she extended the word and added more breath and moisture and warmth. "Get yourself comfortable."

I obeyed and sat and sunk into the lounger, which, just to be honest, I had no recollection of ever sinking into.

She pulled the wooden chair in front of the lounger. I moved my legs apart so they didn't get bumped. She slid the chair in and sat with her back straight and legs crossed and said, "Let's talk about your theories."

I stammered. "Really?"

"Yes."

"Oh."

"How did you come up with them?"

"The count thing?"

"Yes," she said. "Did you come up with them on your own, or did someone point it out to you?"

"I saw the clocks," I said, and pointed to the round-and-round one on the shelf behind her.

She looked up and back and smiled. "Just like that?"

"Kind of. I guess."

She gave me a "hmmm" and took a deep breath, then reached across my thighs, put both hands on the arms of the lounger and leaned in and looked at me, right in my eyes, like she was trying to X-ray my mind. It got me a little twitchy. And I felt stuck in the chair, with her guarding me.

"No one helped?" she asked.

"Well, yeah. Herm. With the car, I mean. That helped with the speed thing. And Susy Liu Anne."

"Susy?"

"Herm's wife," I said. "She gave me the book."

Sophia nodded towards the beer table with the books. "Which one?"

"None of those. The history one that has no history. By that Hawking guy."

She laughed at that, and her laugh was small and chuckly and her cheeks got all balled up and her eyes squinty. Then she leaned back and asked, "What if Time could stop?"

"What do you mean?" Because I wasn't sure if she was still boring into my brain or really asking about Time.

"I guess my question is, really, what if we could stop everyone else's Time?"

"So you believe me?"

She chuckled again. She had a really nice chuckle. "That you thought up your Time theories? Sure, I believe you."

I was trying not to be too excited, but I couldn't help it, not with that sweater staring at me and her telling me to think Time. And it made me dumb. I'm dumb a lot, I realized. And I just stared at her.

She said, "But if you don't want to talk anymore, I understand," and turned towards the window and the tree. "It's dead," she said.

That's when my dumbness broke and I said, "You're not stopping Time."

"I was thinking out loud."

"No. I know. I'm just saying that you're not stopping Time for anyone. You're just stopping everyone else. Like they're all on freeze. And so are their watches."

She paused, thinking, then said, "I guess you're right."

"Because Time's a count, remember?"

And she said, "I remember."

"Yeah." Then we both went quiet. I got to thinking about my situation. There I was with a beautiful woman on the chair between my legs, ruminating about Time, both of us thinking the same theory. Herm wouldn't've believed. I could barely believe it. I was nervous, excited, a little revved up, and even smart—all at the same time. It was the most amazing feeling.

I'm sure I had this humungous grin on my face when she said, "How's your wife?" and slammed the anvil into my face. I felt stupid again, for forgetting the ring that suddenly felt like teeth chomping into my swollen finger.

"Gone," I said.

"You're wearing the ring."

"I'm still married."

"Are you separated?"

"I guess." And I kept sinking into the lounger, into the

dent my ass had made all those years.

She got quiet and started staring out the window at the dead tree.

"She left," I said, "like a long time ago. Months."

Sophia nodded.

I said, "But you saw it before, right?" I jutted my chin at my wiggling ring finger.

She looked up, gave a quick sigh. "Yes," she said. "I did." The wooden chair made for an easy lift of a light body, and before I could even slide forward and set my hands onto the arms of the lounger, Sophia was up and grabbing her coat. "It's been nice."

I swear, that's the fastest I'd ever shoved myself to my feet. And I came up spouting, "She's not coming back. She's not. Really. I know." Unfortunately, it came out this frustrated, pleading whine.

Sophia looked right at the ring. "It's not she who matters."

"I can take it off."

"You don't need to do that."

I don't know if I'd been overloaded with epiphanies or Time thoughts or breast thoughts, but all the sudden I started blabbing and racing my big body between her and the door, almost blocking her. Without my hands though. I didn't use my hands at all. "The books," I said. "We didn't even get a chance to go through them. You want to borrow them? You can take them if you want. I'm the library guy. I'll put them in your name. I've got lots to read. Really. I can't read three at once."

She stepped around me, and I realized what I was doing and scooted the other way. Because I didn't want to block her. Not like that. I was just, you know, a left tackle, and kind of frantic, like I said. An idiot. So I ran and picked up the Mayan books and rushed back and held them out. "Here."

She took one, flipped to the back cover, looked at it for a second then up at me, then handed the book back. And she put on her smile face—that fake one, meant to be obvious so I'd know. "It's very kind of you to offer, but I think I'll check them out myself." Then she headed for the door, opened it, turned around in the doorway and held out her hand to shake. Not even thinking, I shook it, and when I felt the tug away, I dropped it. She said, "You've got a nice theory, Selraybob." Then boom, she'd turned again and was in her car and driving down the street. The cur dog was yapping and I was standing on the stoop, watching her taillights and turn signal and the car round the corner at the end of the block.

I don't know how long I stood there, but the longer I did, the less I could figure out. I'd had my ring on the whole time, so why'd she wait till the last minute? I wasn't the one to steam up her neck and command her down to the lounger. I didn't say anything crazy—just about my theory. And she knew my theory in the clock shop. And she liked it. And what about the backs of the books? What was she looking for? And why Mayan? That was old news, right? Or maybe she wants *Ha*mayan books. Maybe there really is a conspiracy. And maybe she's the center, the

Waketon source of the anti-Time contingent. But dammit, if it was all about the conspiracy, then she never even liked me at all. But I saw it. I saw a glimpse of it unfake. Not long, but for a second she liked me.

Aww, damn, I thought. *I'll never know. Ever.* Because how the hell can you ever know how it is for a woman? Or anyone? If you're not there, sitting in their head and going through all the rejection and laughing and arguments and fears and crap they're going through, how can you know really, for sure? You can't. You can only guess.

And that's what I was doing—guessing, right up until the cur dog went on a yipping streak and I looked over and saw the red Camaro drive up and turn into the driveway. And right there in the driver's seat, all primped up and happy, was Joalene.

23

Maybe I Was Wrong

Joalene pulled her yellow suitcase with the red flower and a grocery bag out of the back of the car, gave me a big smile and walked up the path with her hair curled and swooshing behind her. Her greeting to me was, "What are you doing out in the cold?" And then extra sweet, "Honey...and the door's open."

"Yep," I said.

She gave me a quick pat on the shoulder. "Come on inside."

"All right." But instead of backing in, I turned sideways to let her around, and then I closed the door with her inside and took a couple steps into the yard. I stood getting chilled and watching the road where Sophia'd been and listening to Joalene inside dropping her bags as if she'd been on vacation. And I was thinking how she'd tossed a pet name my way—for the first time since little Lexie died. *Honey*. I was her *honey*. All the sudden.

It was like a universal conspiracy to muddle me all up.

So I stayed outside and listened to the wind gusting around the house and the tree branches scratching into each other and every once in a while my cur-dog buddy barking down the way.

It was the chill in my toes and the thought of them falling off and me falling over that finally sent me inside. First thing I saw was Joalene standing by the lounger and looking down at the chair still in front of it. "Is the lounger broken?"

"Take it," I said. "It doesn't fit anymore."

The words were sudden, not expected, but whiskey, coffee, whatever the chemicals Sophia'd gotten into me— they'd brought up the truth and saved my ass from explanation.

Joalene looked at me, glanced down again at Sophia's chair.

"It's too big," I said.

She gave me the vertical scan. "I can see that. You're almost fit."

Almost again. It would always be *almost*. Even if I was perfect.

She caught my scowl. "No. Sorry. You look fit. Really."

"No. I agree. *Almost* is right. I've got a ways to go."

She hesitated. And I felt it coming. You'd think I'd be prepared for it—the end. Finality. The blood oozing out of my chest and staining the carpet with the last stab.

"That's not why I'm here."

I got the urge to run outside again, to let the cold into my brain, that suddenly felt hot.

"I've got no place to take it," she said.

That was the first prick. Because it was cryptic. Was she moving away? Moving back in? Was there a fire?

"Termites," she said.

I let it all set in, before I finally ripped out a completely unremarkable, "Oh."

She stepped towards me. I stepped back. She stopped. "They were everywhere, Sel. They were in my clothes, and in my hair. It was awful." She wasn't looking right at me. It was an explanation, and that was it. "They have to replace some beams in the floor, and the floorboards too. On my side of the building at least." Only then did she look up.

I nodded. She put on a smile.

"So the lounger stays," I said.

"It stays."

I nodded again. They weren't big nods, like on a bobblehead, but slow and steady. Because I had to move something. About every other part of me was stuck.

"How long are you out?" I asked.

"They haven't said. A couple months. You know where I live…It's old."

But I didn't know where she lived. I'd looked. But no luck. Or at least I hadn't tried hard enough. But at some point during the last few months I'd stopped looking. I almost smiled.

"No, I don't know. Where is it?"

"Susy Liu didn't tell you?"

"No."

"It's not important then."

"And you came here."

"Yes."

She stepped closer again, started to reach with her free hand to pet my shoulder, to ingratiate herself back into my erratic little life.

So I made sure my voice was cold and my words clear.

"What about Mr. Big Round Fixer man."

"Who?"

I stopped at the door. "The clock fixer who looks like a moon. He's got to have a big house."

"Almost fit is about fifty pounds from svelte."

"Hey. I didn't go searching out the roundest guy in Cape G. You feed him lasagna, too?"

"Why do you think I was there, Sel? At the clock shop. Huh? Why?"

She was pissed off, and I was pissed off, and she was always better at thinking when she was mad than I was. I was trying like hell to dig out a good torpedo to blast at her, but nothing came. I was trying too hard. All I got out was, "You tell me."

"To find out about your stupid Time crap—that's why."

"So now you're calling me stupid."

"No, Sel. You're not stupid. I never called you stupid." Right then, as if her bubble of mad had popped, her eyes eased out of their glare and the crease between them smoothed. Her whole body seemed to slump, and she went on in this fed-up but worn-out voice. "He was a professor, Sel. Of physics. He studied. He researched. He even taught a course on Time theory. Three times. But there is no answer. I tried to tell you. The search goes on forever. That's why he let it go and fixes clocks."

"So he quit."

"He learned that you can't live your life chasing fantasies."

"Whippty-do."

I hadn't said *whippty-do* since I was nine. And I don't know where it'd come from. Joalene just shook her head in her disgusted way and turned again and walked into the kitchen while I watched. A few seconds passed before I stormed after her and yelled, "And what about Mr. Hairless Calves, from downtown?"

"He's my new boss, Sel. I had to go."

"Like you had to leave here and like you had to call Reggie and had to buy a new car and had to do your hair up all feminine to come home and show me what I've been missing."

"One, I leased the car. And two, I came home to cook you a pizza. From scratch. Sel..." And she stepped towards me for this, to get close, and brushed aside the hair from her ear so I could see the little ultra-sensitive lobe that used to be, back in the backseat days, the key to her libido. "If you still eat pizza. Or chicken. There's chicken in the suitcase, in a cooler bag."

I stared, flabbergasted.

She said, "And a roasting pan."

"You're going to roast a chicken?"

She smiled. "I can."

I didn't buy it. "In this house? With the smell getting all through the curtains and into the lounger and rugs and everywhere?"

"Yes," she said. "In this house."

"Without puking?"

"I think so."

"Wow." It was amazing. I could almost taste the luscious, crispy, juicy skin. But the craving I'd had during my days on the lounger was gone. "Where are your clothes?"

"In the car. I have a hotel."

"So you're not staying?"

"That wasn't the plan."

"What is the plan?"

"It's in flux."

"Since when did you flux?"

"It's hard to say. I had to settle things out, Sel. Things have changed."

"Yeah," I said. "They have."

She stepped closer—my wife, with her voice low. "You see, Sel, sometimes you have to get out and look around. You need a different point of view. That's the only way to see how things are today."

And maybe living together for so long had melted our minds together a little bit, got us thinking alike even if we didn't know it. Because sometimes you can stare for years at the same clocks from the same chair and all the sudden have an epiphany. But until you shove your ass out of your lounger and given your life a good up-down, inside-outside examination, you don't really see. I got to glancing around. Instead of noticing her apron still hanging on the hook, I saw the oven door that was slightly off hinge and the handles discolored in the middle and the empty place where we were going to put the dishwasher with my moving-man money. And I saw the worn paths on the linoleum and Joalene's scratched-up desk and the stains above the lounger that looked more like a butt really than breasts. The ceiling felt too low, and the whole place cramped. I didn't know how we'd ever fit.

And while I was glancing, Joalene's hand found my neck and was caressing the underside of my ear with the softest fingers—the first fingers I'd felt in years where she'd actually put herself into the touch—I started to realize I hadn't seen her the same either. It was an epiphany.

I said, "Thanks for the lasagna."

"You're welcome."

"But I don't want lasagna. And I don't want pizza or chicken or chicken pizza."

Instead of dropping her hand away, as I'd expected, she reached farther and began to massage the back of my head. "You can have something else. Whatever you want."

I went saggy, like my guts were dropping low and my belly too, and it would've been so easy to take to the lounger again. Because it comes in waves, and this wave was a truckload of want urging me to take to the lounger and relax with a touch. So my thinking stopped, and just like had happened with my lounger comment, that I'd miss like hell, up came what I really meant. "I want Time."

Her fingers stopped massaging. She leaned away. "Your dead-end theories?"

I nodded. She shook her head and closed her eyes. "But you have a good job, Sel, and maybe even a wife and a home." As she pulled her hand away and stepped back, I glanced towards the window, feeling the empty space on my neck where her fingers had been and how pretty Sophia's were, long and dainty, as she'd leafed through the Time books.

I must've looked guilty as all hell, because with a quick glance at the lounger and chair, Joalene started in. "And a girlfriend. You've got a girlfriend, don't you?" Joalene was tense and snarly and her throat was twitching.

"No," I said.

"How long you been cheating? Since I left? That's why you got yourself fit, isn't it?"

"No."

"You couldn't do it for me, could you?"

"It wasn't for a woman." And it wasn't. It was Carl who'd gotten me moving again, and Time that had gotten me out in the first place.

"Dammit, Sel." Her arms went limp and her voice soft again. "That's all I wanted. For you to take care of yourself. That's all. Just for you to make some sort of effort."

"Then you wouldn't've had to leave at all, to find a new point of view. I would've been everything you always wanted. Everything, right?" I pulled myself up and shoulders back so she could see all of me. "Selraybob, the puppy killer—I would've been the *one*?"

That caught her, and she looked down and leaned back against her chair. "I don't know," she said. But she did know. We both did. Every time she saw me, no matter how fit I was or steady I was at work, I was a left tackle and Reggie a quarterback. And that's the way it was going to be. So I looked over to the lounger and at the table beside it and at the books.

"I'd like the dictionary," I said. "If you don't mind."

Joalene snapped, "That's my dictionary." As if her brain was on vibrate between sweet and surly.

"Just the cover, then." I stepped around her, brushing my shoulder against her as I did, then around the lounger to the beer table. And I opened the dictionary and stuck my fat finger between the folds of the paper-bag cover. Without looking back, I pulled gently against the tape. It stuck. I pulled harder. Joalene scoffed from behind. The paper tore, and I looked at the cover and decided that all I wanted was my title. *Selraybob's Dictionary of Science.* I found myself smiling as I yanked and ripped the label from the bag. The Mayan books were beside it and I picked those up. And as I turned with the stack and the brown scrap of paper folded in half, I was grinning.

Joalene wasn't. But not mad either. She was just watching with her shoulders shrugged and head hanging all sad. It killed my grin.

"Enjoy the house," I said.

"I told you, I have a hotel."

"That's your choice." I scanned the house, for what I was sure would be the last time. "It's not mine anymore."

"I don't know that it was ever mine."

I stopped beside her on my way to the garage. "Sell it."

She didn't answer. And we stood there for a few seconds, not talking and not looking at each other but standing close enough to touch, which only I did this time. I said, "I got to go," and I reached and rubbed her arm.

"You don't," she said.

It's a sinker when you go so long without touching and it's not until the last hour that you reach for each other as if you care, because you do care. And you have cared. But you can't stay.

"I do," I told her.

So I turned away and walked to the garage, lifted the door, opened the car door, revved the Corvair, then backed out around Joalene's Camaro, into the grass, and drove towards the cur dog, which had already gone silent. I didn't want to stop or even roll down the window and say, "Hey buddy," because the risk was that I'd slip into reverse and head all the way back to the lounger. The crack-skinny woman was at the gate—she'd probably been listening to us bicker—and she looked at me, and I looked at her, and she looked down at the silent dog at her side. But I forced myself to roll on by. As soon as I was past, the barking started and kept on until the end of the block, where the turn is.

Instead of easing through, I stopped full on and let the

car idle a bit and listened to the cur dog calling. That wasn't a pathetic goodbye, I told myself. It was okay. But I stayed at the intersection, one foot on the clutch, the other on the gas, idling, and forcing myself to look forward. I even caught myself shaking my head and closing my eyes and muttering, "Go, Sel. Go. Make the turn." And then louder, "Aw, Jesus, Sel. What are you doing?"

I jammed it in reverse, looked over my shoulder and started back. As I got closer to the cur I noticed Joalene in the doorway, watching me. And I wondered where I was really heading.

But as I got to the cur dog and noticed the quiet, I knew. I stopped in front of the gate and rolled down the window and said to the crack-skinny woman, "You got a nice dog there."

She said, "He was my husband's," and opened the gate. The dog sprang out and ran around the car, and I leaned over and opened the passenger door. He jumped in and sat up and looked out the windshield ready to go, as if he'd been expecting me.

I closed the passenger door and nodded to the woman. "I'll take good care of him," I told her, and then took one last look back at Joalene. She was still on the stoop with her arms crossed, still watching. But the emotions that had been swinging through her looked gone. More curiosity is what I saw. Until a smile came to my face, a little wistful, a little happy—the kind that comes when ends meet beginnings. The same smile came to Joalene. We held our gazes until my eyes got foggy and I turned back to the cur dog. I scratched his head, told him, "Nice to have you along, buddy." And we headed down the road to follow Time, and whoever and whatever came with it.

Favorite Words
from the
Dictionary of Science

These aren't all the words I learned, and they're not all about science, but for one reason or another, either because they sound cool or because they mean something interesting that I'd want to tell Herm or Susy Liu Anne or Joalene, back when she was around, I'm putting some down.

Commence: To start. That's it—simple. But I like it better than *start*, which is why I stuck it in the first chapter.

Curmudgeon: That old codger guy sitting on his stool and barking about the traffic and the honking and the kids who play kickball in the street. It sounded a lot like *cur dog*, so I looked it up. And I was right. *Curmudgeon* came from *cur*. So if your local curmudgeon is anything like my cur dog, open the door and take him for a drive. He just might like it.

Cynophobia: An abnormal fear of dogs, which is what everyone thought I'd developed after the Lexie death and the piano incident, but it was really the fear of stumbling or slipping or dropping something and killing dogs, or seeing a dog get killed, or even hearing about a dead dog. That was my fear. The cur dog helped me get over it. I think because it was so mangy-looking from the outside that I figured that it'd be smart enough, like cur-dog mutts are supposed to be, that it'd avoid spiked canes, falling pianos and stumbling left tackles.

Epiphanic: When all the sudden, some idea comes up and it's as if you'd never thought of it or no one else has ever thought of it, it's epiphanic. Supposedly, the word came from the sudden appearance of Christ, or some other deity, that you didn't believe was there, and then *poof*, there he is, all bearded and noble. That's how epiphanic ideas are.

Flabbergasted: Beyond belief. So crazy to you at that instant that you're beyond shocked.

Hormone: Now you're going to think I've been reading *Men's Health* or some other back-waxer magazine. I haven't. I haven't even read any of those relationship books that talk about men and women and hormones and all that crap that goes nowhere unless you really do shave your calves and drive a Lamborghini. Hormones are these chemical-type substances in your body that keep everything in check, normally. Like female hormones during that red time of the month or overactive teenage boys always thinking about cheerleaders with full-body giggles. When hormones are out of whack, you're out of whack. So they're meant to keep things regulated. They got me stuck on Joalene.

Iconoclast: A person who comes up with theories and ideas that everyone else thinks are crazy, and may be, but that sometimes are be brilliant. Like Einstein was with relativity (which was right) and the fourth dimension (which was wrong) and Galileo was for supporting Copernicus. They're often spit on and punished and pursued by the armies of the mainstream.

Oblivious: Looking back, this could be the word for my life up until Time. What it means is that you don't have a clue about what you're seeing. There could be a bear in front of your face, and you're so busy thinking about lasagna that you don't see it until it's slicing you open from love handle to love handle. That would be oblivious to the obvious. Or sometimes you see the bear, but you tell yourself over and over again that it's not there, so you kind of convince yourself—even though deep down you never really do—that it's not there. Until it jams its fangs into your temples. Then you realize that you weren't as oblivious as you thought you were. That's kind of how epiphanies are sometimes, except for the blood—all the sudden you realize something that's been staring you in the face all your life.

Paradigm: A cool word. It's all about how you look at things. If you're in the top of a tree and look down, you might see a squirrel and leaves and some bark, maybe even a bird and patches of dirt and grass probably. But if you're looking up, you see bark and leaves, but you see sky instead of the grass. Not that either one's wrong. You just don't see the same things unless you're looking in the same direction from the same looking spot. So a paradigm's a looking spot.

Revulsion: That puke feeling you get when you see an opossum gnawing on a Labrador's leg or a momma in a minimart telling her kid he's stupid. You either got to take out your shotgun or turn away, or else you're going to vomit all over the checkout stand.

Succulent: Dripping down your chin, epiphany-making, moist, tasty goodness. Like the roasted chicken. The mart's was succulent, and the ones Susy Liu Anne made were super succulent—which means the best roasted chicken ever. Herm's a lucky man.

About the Author

Selraybob is a philosopher, writer, and, given his modest Missouri background, one of the least expected deep thinkers on the planet. His theory of time—that Einstein and Hawking and the rest of the spacetime preachers are misguided to the point of lunacy—has invited ridicule and hatred and threats of violence. He has become, arguably, an iconoclast. Selraybob continues to pursue Time, related physics theories, and, with the help of his buddy Herm, Herm's wife Susy Liu Anne, and a small but growing band of supporters, battle the narrow minds of the Time Fixers.

Disclaimer

Permission was neither asked nor given for the use of places and products that appear in the book. And, while most of the people and places described are absolutely real to Selraybob, in some cases, changes were made in order to protect the privacy and security of those institutions, businesses and people. For instance, the folks of NIST. Because they clearly didn't expect to be outed as the Time Fixers they are, they were fictionalized. Any resemblance to any person living or dead is coincidental.